Falling in Love with Paradise

by *L. Elaine*

Acknowledgements

Hi Everyone! Here we are again in the Dynasty of Love series spending time with another brother in the Gutiérrez Family, Javier Roca Gutiérrez. This book is longer than the first one, *Falling in Love with Chocolate.* Why? Those who read Juan Carlos and Lacey's story said "tell us more about this family; who they are and where they come from." I complied as the whole point of love is being connected and in community with others!

Thank you to everyone who helped me with Javier and Olivia's story—there isn't enough space to name all of you. A few shout outs:

One of my sister friend's name is Olivia—I created this heroine to name after her, and I say thank so much for providing me facts and research on her family's home country of Barbados. Barbados is a beautiful place and one of my favorite islands to visit.

The cover idea for this book, *Falling in Love with Paradise,* came from a photo I took of a stranger on a swing in Phu Khet, Thailand. Much thanks to my middle son, Aaron for cover design. He painted the scene from my scant details and anonymous photo. He captured Javier's Olivia in a swing that overlooks the blue ocean; thanks to my oldest son Alex who took the painting and worked his graphic design magic to turn it into 'the cover.'

When I began this book in the Spring 2013, I hadn't written in years. My father passed away suddenly .and I needed a way to be expressed, and deal with the grief. I started writing; the beach scene on Javier's private island just seemed like an unrealistically fun adventure, the perfect escape. Thanks to my football team of brothers, Warriors AC. They were the ones who saved me, let me tag along as their big sister/cheerleader. They shared stories about dad and I got an opportunity to have more family.

A great debt of thanks to everyone who supported *Falling in Love with Chocolate*, read it, purchased it, promoted it, showed an interest in its success and indulged me in conversations about it. Your generosity was a wonderful blessing! To mom, cousin Jean and others for being promoters, I honor you for your efforts. For my friends who shared with their friends, for my hair care dynamo Brenda for setting my book in a corner of the shop—thank you!

Thanks Jen Coken for continuing to compel me to share that I am an author; to Michelle J—thanks for keeping me sane planning to launch. To all my friends, I appreciate your constant support. To my romance reading buddy, Denise—your unwavering support keeps me writing. I apologize if I forgot to thank someone by name—thank you! I love to hear from my readers so please share your feedback on my website: lelaineromance.com

For those want to write, share their creativity or publish a book, I have only three words of advice:

Get To It!

Introduction

"You pierce my soul. I am half agony, half hope...I have loved none but you." ~ Jane Austen, Persuasion

Falling in Love with Paradise, a story of two people, Javier and Olivia, who take a chance meeting and turn it into a worldwide adventure of love that takes them from the beaches of the Caribbean to the countryside of Spain. Neither one of them plans to fall in love, and yet they are also unwilling to ignore their attraction or walk away, even when life's circumstances made it easier to just say goodbye. Olivia, a romance writer, spends all her time writing books of love, yet she is a woman once scorned and unsure if she believes happily ever after is even possible. Then there's our hero, Javier, who is actually a hero who traded in working for the family's olive oil company to save people as a search and rescue pilot. As life unfolds, they discover the value of supporting those you love and how family ties are the foundation of who we've become.

This book begins with two of my favorite islands, Antigua and Barbados. My first time on these islands was on a cruise and I wanted to stay. I fell in love with the people in both places, and their generous spirit. I also love the beaches in Antigua—one for every day of the year; and I adore the diversity of experiences in Barbados from mountain to beach and always with warm trade winds blowing to keep you content and happy. I love travel...sail on!

This book ends in Jaen, Spain on the fictitious family estate. I promised you in *Falling in Love with Chocolate,* I would share more about this big family—here we go to begin our discovery of this proud and hard-working family, it's history and traditions. Read on and continue our journey into La Familia Gutiérrez in book two of the *Dynasty of Love* series: <u>*Falling in Love with Paradise*</u>.

Prologue

*"I need a timeout. Send me to the beach and don't let me come back
until I change my attitude"*
~ Author Unknown

Sitting in the chaise lounge chair of her bedroom, Olivia
Stevenson thought to herself and then spoke out loud:
"this sunny morning – I feel…so-so." *Hmmm, did I say
that out loud*, she wondered? She was never aware if
she was speaking her thoughts or simply thinking them.
It didn't really matter as she was alone watching the
cold rain pelt down. 'Angels were crying when it rains,'
said her mother when she was a child. Mama Jane also
used to say, 'the angels hold you when no one else is
around to love you, and they gave the best hugs.'

Olivia did not believe there was anything that topped a
human hug, especially if your lover was the one giving
them out. What would it be like to have 'the one' you
love holding you while the rain pours down on your
windowsill? Or better yet, to be making love to you as
if there was no tomorrow, nowhere to be, as if you were
the most important person in their world. She sighed
whimsically, "how romantic!"

A short time later, Olivia came back from that
daydream. "Well woman, that ain't what's happening
now and you have a flight to paradise in a few hours."
She took a deep breath. Then another. She looked over
at the half-packed suitcase in the middle the floor. She
stretched, got up from her place and moved to the closet.

She had never liked packing. "I should really hire someone to pack for me. It's not like I can't afford it." She sighed… "perhaps next time."

Packing was at least in action. One could still pack even when their heart was broken. Wanting a hug, loving someone, daydreaming—all those things could be sad. Well today, I am empowered. Why? Because I am sick of pretending like I am some weak victim! I am going to paradise where I can soak up the sun, warmth and sand on the beach all day. So what if the guy I decided to take a chance on loving broke up with me and married someone else? "Olivia, you been down this road before—it is a long story, not worth rehashing the details." He was the one who wanted to be in a relationship with me. I finally gave in, shared all of me with him—my hopes, dreams, fantasies, and it ended. For months, I thought I had done something wrong. That hurt—I hurt. We were friends, I thought. I gave my heart like I never had before. And then to wake up one day and be shut out! It was not supposed to be like that. I was a fool for love! I still remember his last words to me two years ago, 'I want to end our friendship.' We ended our friendship.

Love is a many splendored thing. Yeah right! Who made that crap up? Love is complicated, a hassle, and has one put too much at stake. I am not sure I trust people anymore or myself. Do I pick right? How could it go wrong if they picked you? I am not sure I have yet recovered from loving John Marshall or if I ever will.

Meeting him had been so random, and I was clueless. Looking back on it now, I am not sure what I wanted. Going along with the program cost me something. Being attracted to a man had its own out of control elements to it.

I like control! I am in control of what I do. Not giving my heart so easily ever again. It's not worth it to take the risk of them walking away when it suits them. I cannot trust men with my heart, it is my flaw. Good thing the whole world is not like me, she mumbled as she dropped more stuff into her bag.

Much more exciting to live in a fantasy world! So I write. Writing romance novels has a story turn out happily ever after, even if it does not often happen in reality. This is my one opportunity to go out in the world and create love. They don't have to be like me. I will make a difference, let people know there is love if they want to pursue it; an ability to walk through what did not work, and create a new happily ever after. After three best sellers, that has to be the recipe, the winning formula!

Who am I kidding? She slumped down on the edge of the bed and looked out the window. I don't feel like writing a love story; one can never be sure of how life is going to work out anyway! I am mad, and angry with myself... I am so tired of going from victim to inspired and back to victim again. It happens all too often. One thing for sure, I am not going to have life kick me and keep me down. Olivia thought out loud "it's like getting back on the treadmill after you gain those twenty unwanted pounds. I may not feel like it and out into life I go." She threw the last piece of swimwear in her suitcase, closed the cover and zipped it up. "Barbados, here I come. World watch out, there is a new love story to write, and I am the one to write it!"

Chapter 1

"Life is either a daring adventure or nothing. Security is mostly a superstition. It does not exist in nature."
~ Helen Keller

Olivia hurried through the Antigua airport's bookstore, anxious to pay for the magazines she'd chosen and be on the way to her gate. She heard the last call for her flight to Barbados. There was only this last flight out today and she was not going to miss it. In front of her was woman holding a baby. As payment for her purchases the woman pulled out a traveler's check. Oh no, Olivia thought, "this is going to take too long. I will never make my flight."

Behind her came a deep voice. "If you miss your flight, I will fly you there."

Olivia turned around abruptly. Facing her was this stranger. He looked to be six feet tall, of olive complexion, with jet black curly hair cut just above his neckline, and dark eyes the color of obsidian stones. He was fine wine to her eyes. No matter how gorgeous he appeared, she was ready to give this stranger a piece of her mind. She bit her tongue, who does he think he is? Instead she said aloud, "excuse me, are you talking to me?"

"Si, I heard you say that you will never make your flight. I am a pilot."

Her cheeks immediately turned a deep shade of red. Busted! "I was not aware that I actually spoke aloud. I am trying to make my flight and with this delay, it is looking like I will never make it."

Amusement lit up his eyes as if he knew he had boxed her in a corner. "Yes, you mentioned something to that effect too."

Looking him up and down, she was sure that he was joking with her. Men tried to get her attention all the time. It worked out really well to converse with strangers when one was a romance novelist. You could get new story ideas and great pickup lines to use in later books. Olivia decided to take on being nice, even though she did not mean to come off as nice. "You're a pilot? You don't look like a pilot" she said suspiciously.

Javier smiled. "I am indeed a helicopter pilot for a Caribbean Search and Rescue team." Javier said nothing more.

Olivia heard the announcement that her flight number was now departing. What choice did she have? Stay in Antigua hoping that they'd squeeze her onto the next departure tomorrow. What harm could it be to catch a lift. He was after all going her way. The more she stared at him, the more intrigued she became.

"Excuse me, would you like to purchase those?"

She looked back at the cashier. It was her turn at the cash register. She moved ahead and like an automaton, took out her wallet, handed over her credit card and paid for the items that she just had to have. She heard him clear his throat behind her back. She accepted her card back from the clerk, moved aside and slowly turned around to face him.

"What's your decision? I am going that way." He seemed impatient and irritated. One minute he acted kind and the next minute he seemed like she was a burden interfering with his plans.

Her mind was already made up. "Okay, I'll allow you to fly me to Barbados." She hoped like hell she did not live to regret this decision.

He said "good, I'm Javier Gutierrez."

"Nice to meet you. I am Olivia Stevenson."

He bowed slightly and with a quirky smile, he said "nice to meet you too. Now, let's go!" He turned and walked out of the store.

What did she do in that moment? She nodded, dropped her purchases in her shoulder bag and hurried along.

Chapter 2

"I'm a free spirit, either admire me from the ground or fly with me but don't ever try to cage me." ~Author Unknown

Damn she is beautiful, he thought as he watched her while trying not to break his concentration. He couldn't figure it out, but there was something so breathtaking and enticing about this woman…Olivia. Javier was unsure why he offered to fly her to Barbados. That was the destination of the flight's last call he heard so that is where he was going. He had never done anything like this in his life. He was a man of means, and could fly his helicopter wherever the skies and fuel would take him. He has lots of resources thanks to the continued rise in production at his family's olive oil company back in Spain. With the exception of being with his family when he went home, he spent his time working to save others and avert all out chaos. This Olivia woman, she needed to be saved, right?

She had caught his attention across the store back in the airport. He had been reaching for a candy bar and just happened to look at the woman impatiently standing in line shifting her weight from one foot to the other. It was not her small frame at maybe five inches over five feet, her tanned-red skin, nor her reddish chestnut brown hair messily tied up in a clip atop her head. It was her eyes that stopped him midstride. They were a unique shade of blue with depths that reminded him of the ocean. They were like a mirage and made him stop in his tracks. Were they real? He had moved in closer standing just behind her in line as reconnaissance. It was natural habit and part of his former pilot's training to notice every visual detail of his surroundings. He had given up that way of life for more rewarding endeavors. Yet what he was taught never really stopped being in the background and had saved him and others on quite a few occasions.

When she spoke her dismay at missing her flight, her sultry voice had knocked the wind out of his sails. He'd been so unsure of himself for the first time as a man. All he knew was he had to get closer to her, spend more time with her. It was a convenient turn of events that she was missing her flight. He had a solution. Yet, he did not want her to think that he was trying to hit on her. Was he trying to hit on her? Yes, and he did not want her to know it.

And so here they were…sitting next to each other on his helicopter. Helping her into the aircraft, when he got to briefly touch her hand, that was not enough either. Soon they'd land in Barbados and then part ways. Javier thought to himself, Hmmm, I need a remedy. Maybe a layover in Barbados will give me an opportunity to spend more time with her.

******

Being up in this contraption was spectacular! Olivia had always loved to fly in large passenger planes that deposited one in exotic destinations, and that had been good enough. Until now! The view from the co-pilot seat of this small helicopter was vivid and real. She felt she could at any moment reach out and touch nature beyond the glass. For miles there was nothing but blue skies, Caribbean Sea, and an occasional mass of uninhabited land. She could see the deep coral reefs and schools of iridescent fish swimming just below the water's surface. This is amazing! It was as if she was a child again, in awe of all that the universe might freely offer with no limits. How did I get so lucky as to eye-spy on nature? How did I even get here? Right! You met "him" in the airport, she thought, as she turned slightly to admire the man who did not seem to notice she was onboard at all.

On their walk through the airport, he'd made a couple of phone calls to ensure her luggage would be waiting for them when they arrived at Barbados International Airport. Customs had been an uneventful experience and she was sure it was due to Javier's charm and familiarity on the island. She'd aptly now named him the Pilot!

The Pilot had made small talk with her until they cleared the airport hangar and he'd helped her board his bright orange helicopter. And even while they'd exchanged pleasantries, she was still seething angry that she'd put herself in this position. When he held out his firm and sturdy hand for her to grab hold before she climbed the step, she timidly gave him hers, and they touched for the very first time. It was difficult to accept his leg up. She was independent and did not rely on anyone to help her!

So, in defiance, she used her other hand and the strap to pull herself up the rest of the way. To her dismay, she did notice his rough, sturdy fingers against her soft gentle touch—she suspected he was the kind of man who made you believe he could take care of you. She certainly didn't need anyone to take care of her and she never had! He had simply offered gentlemanly assistance. All too soon, their connection broke and she felt immediate longing to reconnect...a desire to keep holding on.

No, no, no Olivia – do not long for that! Being polite, she murmured 'thanks' and she strapped into her seat. The Pilot closed the door, and went around to the other side to climb aboard. Once he was strapped in, he leaned over to check her straps, and then sitting back straight began pressing buttons. After a few minutes of watching that mesmerizing display, Olivia stopped staring. He turned to her, handed her a headset and gave his only instructions. 'Put this on, and do not touch anything until after we land!' Like a fish out of water, she nodded, and did as she was told. Then as if unsure what to do next, she placed her hands in her lap. Lift off, or whatever it was called, had been a silent, almost sterile procedure.

What should I do now? Stare out the window and think about him. Being guarded and at the same time intrigued about all that was happening in nature without anyone's interference, she observed him. He was sexy and drop dead gorgeous, even more so as he wielded this machine to fly through the air. He obviously had skills and charisma to match. Olivia's body was betraying her with each passing moment. It was as if she had suddenly woke up. *He is just as breathtaking as anything you see out there, and here you are inches away. How delicious!* In that moment, she felt a jolt of need to reach out and touch him. She lifted her left hand slightly from where it rested on her leg and she heard the voice of reason say, *Don't Do It! Don't touch him!* And she dropped her hand back down defeated and confused. She couldn't deny her attraction to him, and yet she wasn't ready to show him the affect he was causing to her body.

Who wouldn't be attracted to him? She reasoned it was because of the lack of sex in her life or so she hoped. Yet, there was something about him that radiated a take charge attitude that had people cater to his every request. She'd even been surprised that she'd followed slightly behind like a puppy dog unconcerned as to where they were going or what to expect next. *You do not chase men Olivia or cater to them! And he is just a man, no different than the last one—you know the one that broke your heart.* With that declaration, she could feel the tension seeping into her shoulders. Breathe! Let it go, she reminded herself. This man was not that one. You are no longer the pushover you once were. Breathe! Let it go…

To cope with all that was unfolding in front of her, Olivia turned slightly to stare out the side window, and wondered to herself: Who is he? What is his life story?

Why does he seem like a loner who is unwilling to fit in, and at the same time willing to help others? In the short time Olivia had been around him, she'd already noticed he commanded respect from every man. And even more unsettling was the fact that every woman had turned to smile as he walked by as if he was royalty—women who acted like they were graced to be in his presence and only wanted a little bit of his attention. *Hell, why are you acting like you aren't a fan? Have you not been secretly staring at him too!*

Oh, that flight suit...it should be banned. It's so form fitting showing off his muscled arms and chest, his tall, sleek build and curved assets! *Focus Olivia! You are not some wanton thot. Out of control in this moment, yes! Reign yourself back in! This is not healthy!* Mentally she had a greater need to stomp out the attraction before he noticed or worse, before she gave in to it.

Time for a self-imposed pep talk! Here goes...

He is not into you.

This is him doing his job.

You are not special to him.

He told you he is a life saver.

You are someone he could help out. You happened to be going to the same place he was already going.

During their walk through the hangar, she had said, 'let me pay you!' He said 'no and don't offer again.' She didn't appreciate that he'd refused to take any money for helping her. She never wanted to owe anyone anything. It was inconvenient when they showed up to ask for payback.

Hmmmm what will the Pilot ask of you to repay his service? Her mind wandered again. *How steamy those sexcapades would be...*

Oh Olivia, stop daydreaming! No matter the price, you are not for sale! Instead of continuing down the spiral that led *Alice in Wonderland* into the dangerous rabbit hole, how about you be grateful! Grateful for the lift, the view and the new experience. Yes, that was it – the answer! She was determined be to grateful at least until they landed safely in Barbados, and then she would never see him again. She sighed.

After calming herself down, she heard on her headset that they were on approach and would land in the next few minutes. Perfect timing!

Crisis of lust averted or so she hoped…

Chapter 3

*"I saw them standing there pretending to be just friends, when all
the time in the world could not pry them apart"*
~ *Brian Andreas*

Arrival in Barbados was just as uneventful as it had been
leaving Antigua's airport. Everyone seemed to admire
the Pilot. They smiled and greeted him with familiarity.
They barely noticed she was there, except they did have
her wheeled suitcase waiting at the customer service
desk. Once she had it in her possession, Javier said,
"where are you staying?"

She hesitated not sure she wanted him to know.
"Ummm?"

"Come now, Olivia." He purred. "Surely you are not
afraid to tell me. Don't you trust me? I just flew you
safely here, and did not do anything dangerous or
concerning, si?"

Her inner voice chimed in. *Si, he does have a point. If he
wanted to harm you, he already had plenty of
opportunity.* Ignoring her inner voice, yet still
capitulating she said, "I'm staying at a place called the
Sandy Point Resort."

He smiled, one of those devastating and charming
smiles that was making Olivia forget everything else.
"Good! As strange as this might sound, that is where I
am staying too! It's such a small world!"

21

She spoke with the greatest amount of sarcasm she could muster. "Really, you expect me to believe that you and I happened to pick the same hotel? And why did you say 'good?'"

"Yes really!" He shrugged. "I keep a room there. It's kind of, what do you Americans call it, a home away from home? Si, that's the term! When I work long days searching at sea or have logged too many flight hours to continue, I go there and catch up on my sleep before resuming duty. It is a great establishment on the west coast of the island, with a beautiful view, good food and a spa. I like it very much. Come, I will give you a ride!" He picked up her bag as if it weighed nothing, then turned and walked in the direction of a sign that read 'Rental Cars.'

Olivia was speechless! Again, he did not ask. He commanded that she leave now, and what did she do? She followed. How does he keep doing this? It's as if she were under some spell. His thick accented voice lulling her into submission. Go figure that she and the Pilot were both staying at the same resort. There were too many ironies between her and this man.

As much as she did not want to admit it, there was no harm in letting him give her a lift. She figured she had nothing to lose unless he was a reckless driver, to which she doubted to be the case considering he was an aircraft pilot with his own helicopter.

His unexplained 'good' still left her a bit unsettled. What did it mean? Good, they could ride together? Good, because she picked a great place to stay? Or was there something else the Pilot was plotting? *Olivia,* the voice of reason warned, *let it be! You know better than to ask questions you do not want the answers to!*

The part of her mind that was determined to have him, now in rare form, piped up! *Would it be rude to sit in the backseat and let him chauffeur us? That way we can watch him with little distraction!* Ugh, we are not sitting in the back of the car! Stop fantasizing about him as if you are on some romantic vacation!

She had been around the Pilot for only a couple of hours and already she acted like a wanton woman in heat. Olivia knew she was losing touch with reality. Talking to her insane inner voice was never a promising sign. She needed some time to herself to think. A few minutes to put her public mask back into place, stabilize her nerves. She would get the upper hand and renew her resolve....until then she had to be a rational woman! Yes, rational? NO AFFAIRS Olivia - you are here to do research and write! Who was she kidding! If he offered her any more of his time and attention, she knew she would take it!

A few minutes later and Olivia was settled into the passenger seat of the rental car. She sat back, breathed in deeply and then exhaled slowly. She turned her head

23

to stare out the window, determined to enjoy the car ride as he taxied her to the hotel. Well, it wasn't a car, it was a Jeep. Not what she would have picked for the self-assured pilot. She would have figured him the showy, fast sports car type who liked attention and for others to cater to his whims. This vehicle was too rugged.

He had been raised well, Olivia was sure of it. He was so tightly controlled, even as he pretended to be laid back. He did not seem to care that he exuded sex-appeal. Her senses were fully attuned to every move he made, and he wanted something from her she couldn't quite put her finger on. Then again, maybe she was making too much of it. It was possible her skills at reading people were off kilter. It had been a long trip and she was tired. The sooner she got to the hotel and checked in, the sooner she could forever rid herself of the Pilot and relax. Then you will...

"A penny for your thoughts?" He said interrupting her diatribe.

He just said something! Oh no! How long had he been talking? She turned from gazing out the window to look in his direction. Gone were the aviator glasses that had hidden his cat-like eyes during their flight. Now he was staring at her with blatant curiosity. Why was he staring at her with piercing eyes? "What?" She said exasperated.

He arched his eyebrows at her, knowing he'd caught her off guard. "I'm sorry, did I disturb you?"

"I didn't hear you, that's all. Please repeat what you said?"

"But of course querida! I said, a penny for your thoughts?"

She didn't like it one bit that he'd called her 'dear' in his native tongue either. And she thought it best to ignore his choice of words, determined not to add any meaning to the next frame of the saying "a nickel for a kiss..." Do you think he wants to kiss you? *Hmmmm how to answer that. No don't think about kissing him. Are you going to answer his question? Don't say too much Olivia!* Yes, tell him what he wants to know. She felt the struggle within herself. She was on high alert, and knew she better be cautious. She answered, "I was thinking about how wonderful it will be to check-in and see this beautiful island!"

He stared back at her as if she had two heads. "Okay, sure!" And he turned his attention back to the road.

Was he trying to challenge her to say something else? No way was she going to be honest and tell him she was thinking about him. His ego was big enough! He couldn't tell she was attracted to him, could he? She'd partially told him the truth. It would have to do.

He kept looking between her and the road. The way he watched her made her feel as if he was learning her every detail, reading her thoughts, waiting on her; and she perceived he was ready to respond to whatever she said next. She could not deny she loved the attention. The way he looked at her, wow! She shivered. *Oh Olivia, he is dangerous to your composure even though you already know he is not going to manipulate you. Men don't outthink smart women! They entice women not to think at all. Stay smart, get back into the game and respond to him.* Okay, I'm ready. "Why are you staring at me Javier? Especially considering you are supposed to be driving!"

In his eyes she could see he was being playful as his lips quirked and he resisted smiling at her. "Well, we are at a red traffic light in case you hadn't noticed. I'm using my time wisely observing a beautiful woman. And I'm trying to figure out why she is traveling alone in paradise." The traffic light turned green, and he again moved them forward.

Olivia could feel the blush rising to her face. Why would he say that of all things? His comment surprised her. He thinks I'm beautiful? She didn't know what to do. She opened her mouth to respond and then thought better of it. Silence ensued.

Breaking into her erratic thinking, he said, "if you were my woman, I would not allow you to take such risks." Then he turned his head back forward.

His woman! Ah this banter, she could deal with! She stared at him with indignation, even if it was only possible to address his profile. "You would not allow me? Surely you forgot that a grown woman does not need permission! Hold on, let me look." She sat forward, and with her right hand, she pulled down the passenger seat's visor, opened the concealed mirror, and moved it to stare up and down at herself for a few seconds. "Yes, I just re-checked, I am grown! I make my own decisions where I go or not. So it's a very good thing I am not your woman. However, even if I were, I would still do as I please!"

"Such protest," he said with a wide grin. "What I want to know querida is why you would not want the protection of your man?"

She rolled her eyes and ignored the honey coating meant to soften the blow of his male chauvinistic words. "These are modern times, and we are not cave people. Men do not rule the planet and women are no longer possessions or property to be controlled. I do not need protection. I've had plenty of self-defense classes and trust I know how to handle myself. Anyway, who said I am alone? I could be meeting my lover here in Barbados." She stopped speaking and then waited for his response.

He did not disappoint her as he immediately responded. "Si you could be, but I don't think you are! Are you?"

Olivia had walked into that trap. She was now careful and in evacuation mode. Is he being sneaky? Is he flirting? Or merely assessing his kidnapping options? *You are being illogical. Maybe, maybe not? Find out why he wants to know.* She decided not to answer the 'alone' question and instead ask her own. "Why do you want to know?"

"Ah, avoiding answering my questions! Yet, you say you do not need protection. What are you afraid of Olivia? Perhaps once you are comfortable with me, you will answer any question I ask!"

Don't bet on it, Olivia whispered to herself. I am not going to be getting comfortable with you! Instead of saying that, she plastered a smile on her face, and quietly said "perhaps."

They were stopped at another red light. She watched him lean back, run his hand through his hair, and stop to rub the back of his head and the curls that fell at his neckline. She could tell he was debating with himself, maybe even suppressing some frustration. He dropped his hand back to the steering wheel and sat forward, straightening himself. Then he turned to look at her. Olivia wondered how long this traffic light would stay red. She saw the flicker of emotion as his keen eyes shifted from playful to reflect a newfound seriousness. "Look, my attempts at small talk have been unsuccessful, si?"

Olivia nodded in agreement, but said nothing.

"I apologize if I offended you. It was not my intention."
He paused. "How about we call a truce, querida?" He
smiled brightly and she saw the sparkle return to his
eyes. "I will be on my best behavior. You have my
word on it." That was the moment the light turned
green, as if the universe were attuned to his commands.
He returned his focus back to the road. Then still
smiling said, "and also, I will answer any of your
questions. What do you want to know?"

Why, why, why was she so taken with his smile. It was
like staring into the brightest moon beam that called one
forward to stand in its light. The shadow of a beard was
starting to emerge on his chin and it made him that
much more devastatingly handsome.

Oh, and he spoke with such promise that he would grant
any request as if he was an open book waiting to be
read. Olivia decided she would take the bait. She
wanted to find out the origins of his sinfully sexy accent.
Plus, she thought it best to stray to safer topics than
male-female relationships considering the way the last
topic went. Finally, she said "Okay, that's fair. Truce!"

"Ask away!" He said as he appeared to await her first
question since their declared truce had begun.

"Where are you from Javier?"

"You noticed my accent, huh? I am from a province in Spain, called Jaen. I grew up in a big familia and stayed until life called me to see the world."

Olivia could hear distance in his voice. It seemed like he left something behind there. Yet here he was in Barbados, half a world away from home. She wondered if it was about a lover or girlfriend who stole his heart? Perhaps he just missed his big family. Something told her not to pry further into his life, so she didn't. What was the next safe topic she could bring up? Work is always a safe topic.

"Why did you run so far away from home?"

"I could ask you the same question!"

"I have a better question. How did you become a pilot?"

He was quiet for a moment, almost pensive. Olivia was not sure he would respond. Then he began again.

"When I was a boy, I wished I could soar through the skies the same as I would watch the birds flying across the olive groves. I had read of great adventures and dreamed of exploring unknown places. My parents were very indulgent of me and my brothers. Any hobby we wanted to take up within reason, they allowed.

"I was a good student and wanted to learn to fly. At first, Mama said no. At ten while my brothers spent all their free time either running through the fields, admiring fast cars or chasing girls, I started reading about airplanes and building models. I am the youngest of six brothers, the bebe, so Papa already knew it was likely I'd survive childhood as my older brothers had. So he allowed me to sneak off to the airstrip where I learned the mechanics of aircraft and how to fly. By twelve, Papa had convinced Mama that it was best to get me some formal training so I didn't do something stupid. Mama reluctantly gave in and agreed to my training. I was an ace and excelled at flying both small planes and helicopters. I earned my hours, but due to my age I could not get my license until I was sixteen. With license in hand, I attended university and studied aircraft engineering." He stopped speaking as if he was not going to finish.

"Please go on," she prodded gently.

He began again. "Our parents wanted all of us to go into the family business, and it never held my interest. After graduating university, I returned home to work with Papa and my brothers. I tried my hand at different jobs in the company and was hopeless. Mama definitely didn't want me to go into the military to fly planes, nor did she want me to give up my desire to be a pilot. She called a family meeting to discuss my future. I refused to attend. Finally, my family sat me down and said it was no use me pretending to support the business. They said

I should go pursue my dreams. Basically, they fired me and they gave me their blessing. So off I went.

"At first, I worked in the aviation industry, and then went on to fly small jets for private customers. That was good for a while, and it did make me lots of money. A few years of that and I got bored. I had no motivation to fly for work anymore. I started to party in my spare time, and actually most of the time. When I was finally sick of being around pretentious and superficial people, I asked to come back to the business. The family said while they loved me, they did not want me back underfoot and moping around. Mama said, follow your dreams! I looked at what might satisfy my sense of adventure and going places unknown. I could not come up with anything.

"Really? The whole world at your fingertips, and nothing?"

"One day a pilot friend of mine talked of the difficulties of getting talented pilots who could stay calm and operate in storm conditions. I asked what he was talking about. He said they were always on the lookout for selfless people to go on missions with the authorities to save lives. I was intrigued, and signed up. I trained for sea search and rescue. It was amazing and I love making a difference while saving lives. The conditions are often intense, but I'm calm under pressure and thrive from the challenge. That's all there is to tell."

Olivia said, "wow, that's impressive!" She doubted that was 'all there is to tell,' but she was learning to let him 'leave it at that.'

"Thanks querida! What else do you want to know?"

She knew that at some point he would expect her to open up, and she was not interested in the payback, so she changed her line of questions.

"Tell me about Barbados?"

"Ah, a safe subject. Very well, so I shall." He began to tell her what he knew about the easternmost island in the Lesser Antilles.

They made small talk the rest of the way. Olivia liked that he had stopped being high handed and bossy. She really enjoyed their conversation and that unto itself was amazing. Soon enough the Pilot would walk out of her life, and she would return to normal...

When Javier pulled the Jeep up to the front of the resort, Olivia felt like she'd gone through a range of emotions. She'd accepted his hospitality, misjudged him, mistrusted him, and all the while been attracted to him. She was ready for a break, yet she was sad too that their time together was coming to an end.

The bellman opened her car door, held out a hand and helped her step down from the vehicle onto the walkway. Before she could go for her bag, Javier had already retrieved it and handed it off to the bellman. He'd also handed off his keys to the valet. Time to move on! She walked into the open lobby and he came up beside her.

"Check in is this way."

She could see the desk in the distance. Abruptly, she stopped and turned to face him. "Javier, you do not need to hand me off as if I am some child! I am capable of finding my way to reception."

"I apologize querida. Just figured I'd help out a damsel in distress."

She laughed uneasily. "I am not a damsel in distress!"

"True, but it sounded good, si? Very well, I shall leave you now. Goodbye Olivia!" And he turned to walk away.

"Wait Javier" she said as she placed her hand on his forearm.

"Si querida, what's wrong?"

Oh why does he keep calling me that! It unnerves me. "I just wanted to say thank you again for getting me here, safe and sound."

"It was really no big deal. Actually it was my pleasure. Take care and perhaps we'll run into each other again." He bowed slightly and coyly smiled.

Yes, please, her inner voice screamed. All she chose to say was goodbye Javier. He walked away and she whispered to herself. Perhaps, we might meet again Pilot Javier. When he was no longer in her sight, she did a ninety degree turn, and went to the check-in counter. Back to work Olivia!

Chapter 4

"The only joy in the world is to begin." ~ *Cesare Pavese*

Javier was sitting in the corner of the restaurant. He was tired and hungry, and had come here for a quick bite to eat. The beat of the music which usually called him to the dance floor, was not enticing. If Olivia were here, she would hold his interest, even though tonight was not the night to act of his desires. Tomorrow's early morning start at 4:00 am was coming fast, and he needed to get some much needed sleep. The waitress had just left his presence after taking his order. Anna or something similar was her name. She asked him what he wanted and in her tight skirt and low cut blouse looked to be offering herself as part of the meal. He asked for sparkling water, blackened salmon, rice and peas.

The waitress smiled again, and he did not. She got the hint. In his free time, Javier would take shots and flirt with the best of them. He would drink most people under the table and then go about his merry way. On occasion, he would have a brief fling with one of the wealthy socialites who wanted to forget about life back home. No strings attached, no regrets, no clingy women wanting a relationship. The next morning, he returned to his everyday life; working and enjoying paradise too! He liked this laid back existence. He'd seen too much heartache in paradise to want it for himself.

The service was pronto with the waitress reappearing with his water, and quickly disappearing. While he waited for dinner, he stared out at the dark ocean water, seeing an occasional jaded light twinkling in the distance. Maybe it was a speed boat, passing ferry, cruise ship or barge moving cargo. The sea is what kept people on this island, whether they be natives, tourists or like him ex-pats looking for some other way of life than the one he was born into. He was grateful he could make a honest living here if he ever decided to divest from the family business. When he had free time and wanted to be alone, he went fishing off the dock, and stared out at the mighty sea. Not this trip!

Turning away from the darkness, he looked across to the dance floor. The party was just getting started: vacationers drinking to excess and enjoying their time away from life's realities. His mind wondered to Olivia again. He had been thinking about her off and on since they'd said goodbye near the check-in desk. I wonder what she is doing? Is she in fact here in Barbados alone? If she was, she didn't have to be. He would keep her company. Her smile was intoxicating. The way she talked to him as if she were annoyed with him, was cute. He could sense she was attracted to him; and the feeling was definitely mutual.

He wanted her, and had yet to work out if or when he would have her. Perhaps he could take off a few days. He rarely ever took leave, never had a real reason to rearrange his schedule. Olivia though might be reason enough to spend a few days in paradise. There were no current emergencies. Scheduled drills in the open water would end at 9:00 am, and then he would be free to come back here versus go home. Yes, that was it, he was going to spend some time with Olivia, if she wasn't frightened away by their instant attraction. Only one way to find out!

Just as he came to his conclusion, the waitress reappeared with his dinner, and he tucked it away. He was now in a great mood and had discovered some newfound energy. Perhaps he should have some dessert, even if Olivia wasn't on the menu just yet.

He asked the waitress for the dessert menu. When she reappeared and he looked up, he also saw that Olivia had just been seated at a table across the restaurant, overlooking the dance floor. Ah, dessert has just arrived!

Hmmm she seems to like the music. I wish I were at her table, he thought. Actually he really wanted to have her in his bed, but perhaps he was jumping the gun too fast (or whatever the saying was). He lifted his hand to call the waitress back over. Upon her arrival, he ordered just coffee. He smiled to himself with smug satisfaction. There is really nowhere I have to be right now, he surmised as he watched Olivia. The view is just perfect!

As time elapsed, Javier sipped his coffee. He admired the way Olivia devoured her meal, starting with the bread, and continuing on until almost all of her food was gone. She must have been hungry too. She certainly was not the typical woman who picked over food or only ate salad. Those women were not the kind of women Javier consorted with anyway. They were boney and lacked the luscious curves that were meant for love making. He preferred a woman who had hips and a generous bust.

Right now, he only wanted Olivia and he'd enjoyed his time watching her without her knowledge. Perhaps if he'd had the courage to approach her when she first sat down, he would be further along in his plan. One thing was for sure, he was now hungry in a whole new way— hungry to taste her lips on his, to inhale her scent, to touch her body to his. Just then Javier got a new idea. Now was the time for him to make his move. Life was looking up...

******

Olivia emerged refreshed from her room after an amazing two-hour nap. She was already loving this resort. They had welcomed her into her suite with an impressive fruit basket and sampling of chocolates. After a needed shower, she devoured all the chocolates, an apple and banana. Then wrapped in the traditional soft terry cloth robe that spoke to the opulence of a hotel, she fell asleep.

Now she was famished and in need of a real meal—consisting of meat, rice and peas or some type of hearty island fare. Her stomach must have heard her, as it grumbled. When was my last meal, I wonder? This is a world-class resort, so surely there must be lots of options. Does it matter? Food now is what matters! She picked up her wallet and left her room. *Yes, go get food, Olivia* her inner voice desperately pleaded.

Olivia walked the path to main reception, purposefully dressed in a gauzy white shirt, tan linen slacks, and low sling-back sandals. She did not feel like going to an establishment that had a formal dress code. With weeks of exploring Barbados remaining she wasn't going to venture far on her first night in paradise anyway. It was best to pace herself. There would be plenty of time to uncover all the highly-rated places to dine on the island. Coming into the lobby, she sought out the concierge. He seemed to be a kind gentleman of older age and looked very distinguished. "Good evening, m'lady. How may I assist you?"

"Good evening sir. Might you tell me where I can have a quick and easy meal on-site?"

"But of course. I suggest the patio restaurant. It's called the Calypso Grill," he said as he pointed her in a direction that looked to be towards the beach.

"Thank you very much," she said with a smile.

"It is my pleasure. Enjoy dinner m'lady."

"I will. Have a good evening." And off she went.

As she approached the restaurant, she could smell barbecue cooking and hear lively music playing in the background. It made one want to move their hips to the beat. She couldn't quite tell whether it was Soca or Calypso, but it sounded great and would provide entertainment during dinner.

The hostess at the entrance asked, "how many?"

Olivia said "one for dinner please," and held up her index finger just in case the woman could not hear her over the loud music.

The woman smiled, picked up a menu and said "please follow me, m'lady."

Olivia did as instructed and was led to a small table for two at the edge of the deck. It was a vantage point that allowed Olivia to watch the steel drum band and dancers on the patio below. Eat and be merry!

The service was prompt. No sooner than she sat down and the hostess disappeared, the waitress appeared. She was carrying a bottle of water and a basket of bread. Yes bread! The heavens shine down on us! Remember your manners, Olivia.

"Good evening. And thank you!"

"You're welcome m'lady. My name is Carissa and I will be your server this evening. May I get you something to drink from the bar?"

"Yes, I'd like a wine spritzer, please." On an empty stomach, Olivia knew enough not to get carried away.

"Very good, I'll be off to get your drink, and right back to take your order."

"That will be wonderful!" Olivia watched the waitress turn the corner before she picked up her knife, and opened a pat of butter. She reached for the precut mini slices of French bread and buttered a piece with patience she clearly did not have. Then she put the whole piece of buttered bread in her mouth. Yummy! This is tasty, she thought. Anything, even cardboard would be good to eat right now. However, one can never go wrong with bread as a starter! She ate another piece and then went about studying the menu.

The waitress returned to the table and placed her drink before her. "Are you ready to order?"

Olivia shook her head to indicate a yes.

"What will you have?"

"May I have the roast chicken with rice and peas?"

"Yes, of course. That is one of our most popular local dishes."

"Wonderful! I want to try local specialties, and I am hungry too."

Carissa nodded and said, "Very good. Any appetizers?"

Olivia said "no thank you. Not tonight."

"Very good. I shall return." Carissa took Olivia's menu and off she went.

Olivia was surprised her dish showed up a short time later and she ate every morsel. She was contemplating whether or not to have dessert. She'd learned as a child not to waste food. After eating a whole basket of bread, a quarter of chicken, rice and peas, and a cocktail, she was full. Even as good as the idea of dessert sounded, there was no point in continuing to stuff yourself once full. So she opted for coffee and ordered that instead.

Carissa, ever the lifesaver, brought black coffee and a cup of cream. Olivia added her two sugars, one teaspoon of cream and slowly stirred. As she cupped the mug in her hands, she inhaled the scent of coffee. She calmly exhaled, and tasted a sip of the strong brew. She was mesmerized—better yet, she was enchanted. Life couldn't get much better than this. A hearty meal, beautiful view and the ability to happily watch the party play out on the crowded dance floor below! People seemed so engaged in having a good time, with not a care in the world. If only life were that simple all the time. She sighed.

Olivia saw a shadow cross her line of vision and she assumed it was Carissa coming back with the check. Then she heard a male voice. That can't be Carissa. She looked up to see the Pilot standing next to her table.

"Dance with me, Olivia!"

It was indeed him, Pilot Javier. His approach definitely caught her off guard! "Good evening Javier," she said as she smiled politely and took in all of him in a quick assessment. He was wearing tight jeans and a baby blue polo shirt. This was a surreal moment. He looked delicious, but when had he not! Olivia was still wondering what it would feel like to be held in his arms, kissed by those lips. Did she dream him up? She briefly closed her eyes, took a quick breath, and reopened them. Nope, not a dream. He's still here!

"Dance with me Olivia," he repeated.

Should she pretend that she did not hear him over the music for a second time? That would be rude. She was so tempted to ignore him and yet she wanted to dance with him too. Not a good idea Olivia – you are not thinking straight. *What harm is one dance or two? Stay*

strong and let him dance with someone else. Okay, fine!
She said, "I appreciate the offer but no thank you."

"Por favor querida. Please, just one dance? The music
is so inviting, and I do not want to dance with a stranger
who might get the wrong idea. I want to dance only
with you!" He held out his hand to her.

Olivia was having a hard time understanding what he
was talking about. She was a stranger, and what idea
did he want her to get? Did he really want to dance with
'only' her? Was he using her to entertain himself, or
pass the time away and not be alone? Was he attracted
to her like she was to him? She couldn't decide the right
answer. Yet again though she found herself giving in
and agreeing. She placed her left hand in his
outstretched hand and got up from her seat. "Very well
Javier, one dance."

"Perfecto! Si one dance, you have my word." And he
led her onto the floor to partake in the dance party.

He started to move in rhythm and Olivia followed. She
had learned how to dance to Calypso and Soca music
during her summer travels to the Caribbean a few years
earlier. She was not concerned about the dance moves,
but she was worried about dancing with him. He met
her eyes with every move and turn. It was like they
were the only two people on the floor. Or at the very
least that he only had eyes for her. She was in over her
head, and she knew it as she continued to sway to the

music.   He was a natural dancer, smooth and in command. The fast-paced music mellowed as the band switched to a softer reggae song.

Javier pulled Olivia into his arms.   Wait, her brain registered. One song is over. Technically it's not over, as the music never stopped, so keep dancing. Olivia was beyond caring…she was alive and yet content to be in his presence.   He held her right hand with his close to his heart and she put her left hand over his shoulder. They slowly moved to the beat of the music and for the first time ever she enjoyed the sensation of being led by a man.   She felt her heartbeat racing and the heat emanating off their bodies. She didn't dare move lest he might drop his arms from around her. Dancing so close was the most intimate experience she had ever had with clothes on.   All too soon, the song ended, and Olivia wanted Javier to lay her down right here on the dance floor and make love to her. As if dazed, they both heard in the background the fast-paced music pick up again.

Javier stepped back from her, and immediately she felt a cold chill. "Thank you Olivia for the dance.   It did not disappoint me. Actually, you're a great dancer."

"You're welcome. It was very nice."

Other couples started to move in on them. Javier took her by the hand and led her back to her table. He held out her chair so that she could sit. She let go of his hand, and sat down.

"May I sit?"

"Yes, of course" and she gestured to the seat across from hers. He sat down and looked back over to her.

"Where did you learn to dance like that? You were amazing!"

Olivia blushed unsure of what part of their dance to which he was referring. "I was in the Caribbean once during Carnival and my friends taught me."

"Wow!"

"You are a good dancer as well. How does a man raised in Spain, know anything about Latin and Caribbean dance."

"Ah, my mama taught me."

"Really?"

"Yes, Mama and Papa used to go dancing all the time. It was their special time away from us crazy boys. On rainy days when we were stuck in the palazzo, she would play all kinds of music. Papa was out working, and she needed dance partners. So we learned. My oldest brothers used the skills in the dance clubs to attract the ladies. Probably not what Mama intended. We always have fun as a family. I was one of the last at

47

home with Mama. She would read to me and I'd be her dance partner."

Olivia wanted to ask more questions, but Carissa reappeared and ruined the moment. "Would you all like another drink from the bar?"

"Yes," they both said as the same moment.

Olivia laughed. "Javier, what do you want? My treat."

"Really, whatever I want?" The innuendo was there as if she might be on offer as well.

She stared back at him as if Carissa were not there. "No, not whatever you want! But good try." In a direct tone, she said "now, what do you want from the bar?"

"Touché querida! I'll take a Banks Beer."

"Thank you" she said to him. She turned to Carissa who seemed amused. "The gentleman will have a Banks Beer, and I'd like another wine spritzer, please. Also, the check too as it's getting late." She'd said that more for Javier than the waitress.

"Yes, m'lady. Be right back." And she was gone.

"The service is amazing. It's like they anticipate my needs before I even know them myself."

"I told you this was a great place to stay."

"Yes you did! And you were right."

"So what did you do with your first day in paradise? Take a swim? Go sightseeing?"

Olivia giggled out loud. "You don't want to know."

"Yes I do! Tell me?"

"I took a nap! Well actually I took a shower, ate some fruit and all the chocolates in sight. Then I took a nap."

"Well you do look refreshed and of course beautiful! So it sounds like the perfect day in paradise."

"Thank you for saying that I'm beautiful. You are too kind Javier."

"I do not say this to you as a kindness. It is the truth for me. You are a beautiful woman, and I like being around you."

Olivia turned red. No one had ever been so direct in complimenting her. She did not know how to respond. Not knowing what to say was becoming commonplace with him. He turned her world upside down.

Of course that was the moment when Carissa brought their drinks. She smiled and offered her thanks again.

49

She stalled for time while signing her dinner and the drinks to her room. She could sense his eyes on her. Sure enough when she looked up he did not look away.

"You are at a loss for words querida?"

"Yes. I am not used to someone with your candor." She sipped her wine spritzer looking for some liquid courage.

He shrugged. "I tell it like I see it. I like the company of a beautiful woman. And make no mistake you are beautiful."

"Oh so I am just another beautiful woman destined to be company for you?"

"I did not say that. Please do not put words in my mouth." He took that moment to drink from his beer.

"I did skew what you said. I apologize. I do not want to be treated as if I am some piece of meat for your entertainment or pleasure."

"I would never use you or any woman. I am interested in giving and receiving mutual pleasure. I promise you I am a gentleman always querida."

"Good to hear. I will hold you to that."

"Would you like to take a walk?"

"No thank you. And it would not be a good idea to sleep together."

"Wow, that was bold and direct. Look at you! Who says I am trying to sleep with you?"

"Aren't you?"

"Querida, don't get me wrong, if you were offering I would not turn you down. I am attracted to you. But I think it would not be appropriate, at least not tonight."

"I could not agree with you more. Now, it is time for me to retire for the night. Thanks again for the dance."

"It is I who thank you for a lovely time. Not only did you indulge my desire to dance with you. You also invited me to sit, and bought me a drink. It has been a pleasure. Might you want me to escort you safely to your room? I promise, I will not attempt to come in."

"No, I'll be fine." He then stood and came over to help her out of her seat. He looked deeply into her eyes. "Very well. Good night querida."

Olivia got up, and with her last bit of willpower, she said "goodnight Javier." She turned and walked away. It was such a hard thing to do. She could've talked to him all night. She could've let him walk her back, but then she would not take the chance she'd have the willpower not to invite him into her suite.

Once back into her suite, she washed her face, put on her pajamas and climbed into bed. She thought about her day and meeting the devastatingly handsome Pilot. What shall we say about today? Eventful, yes that was a good adjective!

Chapter 5

"Once in a while, right in the midst of an ordinary life, love gives us a fairy tale." ~ Author Unknown

Olivia had made it to a quiet beach called Paynes Bay, and had already been there a couple of hours. It was also located on the west coast of the island not too far from her Sandy Lane resort. After inquiring into good beaches for one to get away from those who 'want to be seen,' the Concierge said this was the best choice—a place where one could have fewer 'disturbances' still with service (i.e. drinks on demand). She'd found it easily enough on her walk using the straightforward directions. Upon arrival, Olivia had even purposefully distanced herself from the entrance to this paradise in hopes of getting in a morning of uninterrupted writing (or so she planned).

This western end of the island was also known as the platinum coast with expensive villas, yachts, luxury accommodations and seclusion. Olivia didn't much care for the pretentious lifestyle but she did love the amenities and customer service that catered to their money. Her resort's pools and beach were great and also a part of the playground to the rich and famous, with every luxury. Yet, it held 'too much distraction.' If she was being truthful, she was only avoiding one distraction, the Pilot.

Last night was a close call, and she didn't want to again be tempted to give in to Javier's charms. Olivia had no clue what had gotten into her, as she rarely ever paid attention to the advances of men. Friendship first before falling into bed was the key for her. Even at her weakest, she was definitely not a 'wham bam thank you ma'am' one night stand. He was a stranger and she knew little about him, his background, his family, etc. Yet there was something about Javier that turned her on—she went from zero to a hundred in about ten seconds. Could it be that she was still grieving the end her relationship with John? Or could it be that she had not had any company, friend or otherwise, for a long time? Wanting the Pilot was not a good state of mind, even if her body was all for it. Olivia knew it would only end up in heartache, and that was a feeling she never wanted again. She needed to resist the attraction. One sure way to resist was not to run into him again. Looking around through dark sunglasses, she whispered "mission accomplished!" Her inner voice said *excellent, so please now can we finally enjoy the picturesque beauty of Barbados!*

Looking out over the scene, Olivia confirmed it was wonderful here. The beach staff had set up a lovely chair and umbrella for her and were rewarded with a good tip. She hated being sunburned so she'd already applied her SPF 45 twice, and had another cute little umbrella drink on the table she could sip from at will. The bar tab was established and the servers knew not to bother her if there was still something in her cup. When it was empty, they showed up with a new one using the same liquor base. She gratefully signed for it, they politely smiled, said "thanks mi'lady," and disappeared.

How lucky could a girl get in this pure heaven...calm water, white sand, sunshine and the occasional couple walking by looking to be in love. In love with each other, in love with the sun, in love with the water, in love with the sand....it didn't matter. They were in love in life, or so it was easier to believe and craft the next scene. She watched those passing by and time moved along.

Truth be told, even in this idyllic oasis, writing was not going so well. Every few minutes, daydreams of Javier kept infiltrating Olivia's thoughts. What would it be like if he were here with her? What would it be like...to walk with him hand in hand? To play with him in the ocean waves? To touch her hands over his sculptured body? To rub sunscreen over the planes of muscle she'd seen through his flight suit? To have him on top of her....

Get a grip Olivia! You are the author who creates the stories, not the one who stars in them. Right! She chastised herself for her wayward thinking. Coming back to reality, she stared down at the mostly white page which contained two sentences. It has never been this hard to write before! Her English professor always said a romance novel writes itself once the author creates the characters; and one has to be willing to let the story be told!

Focus Olivia, focus!

Okay, she said gently shaking her head to get clear. I'm ready and focused! "His name is Paul; hers is Anna" she said out loud.

Yes, her inner voice said. *You wrote that before. What's next?*

Hmmmm, what direction should I take this book? She mused...

Big city? Yes.

How should they meet? A connection of friends? Maybe.

Olivia's thoughts wandered again...perhaps the couple could meet on this beach. It is so pretty here, and romantic. And then she imagined Javier, one hundred feet in front of her. He was the perfect specimen to star in her love story. What would he look like running along the water's edge? Take 1, Action!

Olivia was right there in the scene, walking along slowly on the sand, allowing her feet to be caressed by the water's gentle ebb and flow. She felt the buzz as he ran by? Who is that? She could see strong muscled legs bronzed in the sun as she watched her fantasy unfold. He was shirtless, in shorts that covered a rear end that wanted to be grabbed? Sweat ran down his back—a clear sign that he was exerting himself in the heat. She couldn't see his face. The playful curls of his hair

56

danced in the breeze and muscles flexed with each stride. He was powerful in life, that was for sure. And he had a magnetism that made her wish she was running alongside him to keep up.

Oh my, she was getting hot. With each move he made, she continued her perusal of every detail of his body she could see and imagine.   She watched until he disappeared. Why had he kept running? Why did he run away from her? Wait!   Wait! Wait! She was clearly dismayed. Her inner voice said, you should have said it sooner, or tripped him up, then we could have gotten a better view of all of him! What if he is the one and you'd let him go without even a hello! Be optimistic Olivia. Maybe he'll run another mile and then turn back around. Yes, perhaps he will!   The daydream continued....

Maybe in running towards you, your eyes will meet his. You'll smile. He'll smile back and then stop in front of you to say he felt unsettled and compelled to run back to find you as if fate foretold a new story...

Earth to Olivia! Yo, Olivia, come back to reality! Why must she come back from such a vivid daydream? Okay fine! Olivia was sweating. It is so hot here! She picked up the magazine and began to fan herself with frenzied effort. Her little voice came right back: *this is pointless! Stop pretending to write. Stop lying to yourself. You wanna have sex with Javier.* Noooooo! Yessssss...I don't know! Ugh! I really don't know. Maybe I do want to sleep with him. She did not like that she was waffling. It's not a good idea, so you are not going to sleep with him!

Her little voice chimed in yet again: *right, even if we are having a weak moment, he is not here, so it's not happening now!* She felt an immediate sense of loss even though she knew it was for the best. She sighed, dropped the magazine back on the chair and set her portable laptop aside!!!!!! The annoying voice in the back of her mind said on loudspeaker, *logic prevails...finally. What now, oh brilliant one?*

She thought for a moment. I know what will work! If all else fails, have a drink! She leaned over to grab old faithful. This time she had a Pina Colada with a chunk of pineapple along the cup's rim. A cold drink (i.e. alcohol) never disappoints! After a few sips, she was happy or at least sated. She sighed. This is a good life!

Pep talk time: *Let's try this again, Olivia. You are here to write! You are a writer who writes effortlessly. Olivia how about you close your eyes a few moments, get a clear perspective?*

Yes, that is sage advice. She did just that, and fluttered her eyes closed. She inhaled a deep breath and started counting silently to herself. Breathe Olivia!...1-2-3-4-5...peace washed over her so she inhaled and exhaled slowly. Keep counting...6-7-8-9-10.

******

Is that her sitting like a goddess perched atop a beach chair? Javier cupped his hand above his eyebrows to get a better view and block out the sun's glare—ever apparent even with dark shades. Lo and behold it is her! Over there under the umbrella, in the cute jade colored bikini sipping some tropical drink as if it was quenching a never-ending thirst. It was Olivia herself, a vision of loveliness.

In the moment, Javier smiled a devilish smile. Oh how the gods had shined down on him. She is like honey nectar waiting for a bear to taste. And he was just the one to sample. "Let's get close to her again" he whispered as he moved towards her in a slow saunter. Never mind she may not want the intrusion. He wanted to know what her lips would taste like and if she would moan his name at the height of ecstasy. He felt the immediate press of his erection straining in his swim trunks. Whoa, slow down! Get a grip. She seems to be a nice woman so don't get carried away. You might scare her.

Practically speaking though, he did want to spend more time with Olivia. Last night she had basically ignored him. He was not used to being ignored when he wanted attention. And most of the time, he didn't want that clingy attention that so many women offered. There was something mysterious about her: the way she'd appeared in his world and then seemed content to disappear as if he was nobody special. She dismissed him and went on her merry way. Well, he was worth noticing. He wasn't going to beg, and still he wasn't ready to back down from the challenge. He sensed she was playing it cool, yet her eyes said come hither.

One thing for sure, she had not shared much about herself. in his opinion that was abnormal as most women never stopped talking about themselves. It made her even more enticing. Far be it from him to pry, even though he was curious why such a beautiful woman was traveling alone. Again, it was a lucky break for him that he didn't have to tolerate other people who might complicate his getting to know her better. He was going to get into her world for a few days. See where it took them, perhaps to his bed. Time to execute his plan of attack on her power to resist him.

"Fancy running into you here." He said as he stopped in front of her beach chair and pushed his sunglasses atop his head.

******

Olivia opened her eyes and there he was. Was she dreaming? Were her non-prescription sunglasses deceiving her? Awareness came over her as if her body knew it was him even before her mind registered it was the one and only, Pilot Javier. She felt the stirring of sensation and the flutter of excitement. Had she dreamed him into reality. That would be some power. Likely it was no coincidence. "Are you following me?" She said with a grimace.

"Not at all." His grin spread across his face. "We just seem to end up running into one another."

"That seems improbable! Is this Island that small?"

"Yes and no. If people move in the same circles, stay in the same general area, it's predictable they run into each other. And if people go to opposite ends, they'd rarely see one another."

Olivia just stared back as him. He was casually dressed with a white polo and ocean blue swim trunks. He is easy on the eyes. *Don't act like you haven't been dreaming about him all morning. Matter of fact, as unnerving as it is, you've been dreaming about him often since you both first met. Find out what he wants!* Olivia opined, "yes, you are probably right. Well anyway, it was nice of you to stop by and say hello. Have a nice day!"

No, no, no, don't make him go.

"Gracias Senorita! But I was thinking I could hang out here with you for a little while."

"Here?" She pointed down to the sand next to the chair. "With me?" And she pointed to herself.

"Si, acqui!" He said with an open wave of his hands.

She raised her eyebrows. He is bold. Two could play the same game. "What if I say no?"

"It is a public beach!! This chair next to you is empty, so why not here. Are you waiting for someone querida?"

She didn't address his inquiry about waiting for someone. She just wanted him to go away, maybe. "Yes the beach is public," she gestured with her hand spread out as he had done, "…and there's plenty of it for you to go off yonder" she said as she extended her arm, and looked around and then back at him.

"Why would you want me to be alone when we know each other?" He shifted his weight from one foot to the other. Had she actually seen aggravation and impatience in his stare?

"We do not know one another!"

"Look, we called a truce, remember? What's the issue in me sitting in a chair a couple of feet away? I am harmless and don't bite." He paused as if to think about his words. He smiled with those charming eyes that crinkled at the edges and continued, "well let me rephrase, I won't bite unless you invite me to do so."

She huffed. "Really? I don't believe you just said that! Well don't look to me for permission. Truce or not, I'm not inviting you to sit next to me! I have work to do."

"That's perfect, we'll be quiet company for each other and no one will bother us. You work, and I'll be the perfect angel. I promise. I want to work too—on my tan!"

She couldn't help but peruse his already tan body from head to toe. From his broad shoulders, and muscled arms that bulged through his polo shirt. She could feel her resistance faltering. What is it about this man? "You are incorrigible! Fine, sit there, but don't expect me to pay any attention to you."

"Gracias querida," he said as he meticulously spread his towel, then sat and stripped down to just his swim trunks. He laid back with not a care in the world. And all the while he said nothing.

Fine! She wasn't going to say anything either.

Olivia picked up her laptop. The movement awaked the screen right where she'd left off before. She just stared at the page. *Oh gosh, if you thought you were in trouble before when you'd been daydreaming about him, now with him here in the flesh and with so much of it on display, you are headed over the cliff without a parachute!*

She sighed and with all the willpower she could muster, she blocked him out and began to type.

******

Olivia was restless. She was staring at the half-written page displayed in the center of the laptop. In the corner of the screen it said 10:30 am. It had been thirty minutes since he showed up or better yet, pulled up a chair and parked himself. She could not concentrate on anything. Laying here next to him at the beach had truly sent Olivia's common sense and sanity over the edge. He'd removed his shirt and sunglasses before he'd leaned onto his back. He was face up letting the sun rays beam down on him. It had bronzed those exposed areas of his skin a deeper golden brown hue and sweat was glistening off his chest. His eyes were closed and he was seemingly asleep.

What am I supposed to do with him, with this attraction that simmers on a slow burn for him? This is an uncomfortable moment. What does he want?

Her brain said well what do you want? I mean you write about tawdry affairs set in exotic locales where the hero sweeps the heroine off her feet. Yet, all of it is made up—every scene crafted from watching snippets play out in front of you. Then you add fantastic story lines to characters who are too good to be true. Is that what this is? A fantasy affair you want to act upon?

Her attraction to Javier was not her dream come true no matter how gorgeous and attentive he was. She was used to simple small-town, boy meets girl relationships. This was a world away from that. Anyone who owned their own helicopter and came and went as they pleased, was not small town. This international playboy was certainly not in her league. But oh how delicious he looks as he melts in the sun.

Looking for a distraction from her thoughts and secretly staring at him, she saved her work. She set her laptop aside and cleared her throat so he would hear.

Javier opened his eyes, turned his head and stared up at her with curious eyes that squinted in the sun. "Si querida, how can I be of assistance?"

"Sorry to bother you," she said, even though she wasn't. "I thought you were asleep and you are sweating, so I wanted to make sure you don't burn. Do you want to move your chair under the umbrella? Do you need sunscreen? Or do you want a drink?"

"Gracias, I'm fine. I'm used to the heat and applied sunscreen before I arrived."

"Oh okay. Good!"

She watched as he turned his entire body onto his right side and leaned up on his elbow. "Yes, I'm good. What are you working on?" He nodded his head to gesture towards her laptop.

Her eyes followed his. "Oh, that! I'm working on my next novel."

"Oh? Are you a writer?"

"Yes, I am."

"What do you write about?"

"I am a romance author, so I write about love."

"Oh so you write, publish and share scandalous stories with people?"

"Yes." She didn't like that he kept asking questions, but she was the one who had awakened the sleeping beast, so she'd tolerate it. At least for a while.

"How did you become a romance novelist?"

"It's a long and complicated story." Why does he want to know?

"I have time!"

She sighed and twisted her hands together as she decided if she would share the whole saga of her life or just the highlights. When she looked over at Javier, she saw nothing but care and concern in his expression. He had told his career story. Now it was time to tell hers, including the back story of how she'd grown up.

"Okay. My parents were killed in a skiing accident when I was three, and they had no living relatives. I was then an orphan."

She saw his immediate frown, and she didn't want his pity. She didn't want his care and concern either, but not many people ever asked her what she wanted. Not his fault. Fair play had her continue.

"I was placed into foster care as a little girl. With a mom who was black and a dad who was white, I was labeled a child of mixed race. Not really what people were into at the time, I suppose. I moved through some number of homes till I was eight. Then I was sent to Jane. She had to be in her sixties when I arrived on her doorstep. At least she seemed old to me at the time. I asked and she said it wasn't polite to ask a lady her age. Jane was a groovy, eclectic spinster! She'd referred to herself as a retired secretary who had worked hard, wisely invested her money, and now enjoyed life."

Olivia smiled. "Little did I know until after her death, she came from 'old money.' Her parents had left her money, and she never used any of it. We lived in a small area in New Jersey called Piscataway. The Victorian house was just outside the college town of New

Brunswick and thirty minutes from New York City. Jane had even named her house, Jane's cottage."

"A Victorian style house seems kind of big to be called a cottage."

"I know, right! Jane didn't seem to care much for other people's opinions, so she pretty much did what made her happy. When I first went to live with her, she told me her parents had named her after a quiet rebel, a woman of great courage—Jane Austen. I was intrigued and asked many questions. Who was this Jane Austen? I learned of Austen's life, great writings, and read all that she penned.

"After a year or so in Jane's cottage, Jane adopted me as her daughter. She said I never had to search again for a family as now I would always have her. I asked if I could call her mom, but she insisted I continue to call her just plain Jane. I am grateful for her. She was wonderful and taught me how to be part of a family and also how to be a good citizen, neighbor and friend.

"Jane was always fiddling with something or working on some project for the local community. Yet, her real passion was reading and drinking tea. It's was a hobby of sort, she used to say. So I learned how to read and drink tea too."

Olivia chuckled. "Jane always preferred a tawdry romance novel much more than writings of social consciousness, suffrage and the women's rights movement."

"Not you though?"

"Nope, not me. However, she indulged me in reading whatever I wanted. I read a few romance books to partake in her genre of interest, but the women were never really independent. They seemed so needy and that was not who I identified with, so instead I found books with strong heroes and heroines as characters. I traveled the world in books and discovered new places to be seen. It was the perfect home for me."

Olivia pondered her next words. "I guess I was good company and we got along well all those years. Jane had never married, and kept to herself for the most part. She too had no remaining living relatives. I look back on it and it makes me sad. Except me, there was no one to give her the kind of love her generous spirit deserved."

"I'm sorry that made you sad, querida. I have always had a big family, so I can only imagine how hard it is not to have family."

"Yes, I suppose you wouldn't know with so many siblings. I had Jane. That was enough at the time. Anyway, Jane repeatedly reminded me it was important to do well in school so I could get a scholarship to college. She'd say, after college I could decide what career I wanted to pursue, and go be it. I really had no idea what to do with my life. I didn't have dreams. I wanted to survive. I wanted to stay with Jane always. I often talked with her about my practical plan to make lots of money so I could open an orphanage for other children with no living relatives. In living there, all the children would forever be a family with me and Jane. I guess it was as close to a dream that I'd allow myself to have. Jane liked the idea..."

Olivia stared out into the distance. The depth of the ocean was ever intriguing, always calling for her to return to its edge. So peaceful on the surface, so strong just beneath. She almost forgot she was telling the story of her first remembrance of heartbreak. She looked over at him. He seemed to be patiently waiting for her story to move forward.

"My favorite place to go was the library. It was research central. By fifteen, I was writing short stories and was an honors student. Jane and I would spend some of our weekends entering writing contests to win scholarship money for college. We had fabulous fun with it. I won a number of those contests and each time we celebrated with a special tea ceremony. Jane would also reward me with a gift card to my favorite bookstore. I saved all those gift cards for a 'rainy day,' as Jane called them. She thought I was crazy and would say, 'stop waiting to be sure instead of living life fully now!' Still, she never pushed me to spend my gift cards. Jane just offered 'wise woman wisdom' I could take or leave."

"I don't mean to interrupt, but I'm curious. Do you still have those gift cards saved up?"

"Yes, they are special to me and there's not been a rainy day yet!"

"Makes sense. Please go on with your story."

Olivia sighed again as this was the hard part. But a promise was a promise. She began again. "In my senior year of high school, as a thank you to Jane, I secretly began writing a romance novel that I would present to her the day of my graduation. My English teacher, whom I'd asked to edit it, said it was a really good story. She recommended when I turn eighteen, I enter it into a writing contest with the local chapter of Romance Writers of America. She outlined that if it was published, it could pay for more than college; it could be my entrance into a career field as a writer and accomplished author. I never cared about publishing it. It was Jane's gift, but I did want the money in the bank for the next 'rainy day.'

"I turned eighteen about four months before graduation. My teacher helped me submit the manuscript. We had the address listed as my teacher's home so it would not ruin Jane's surprise.

"In the meantime, I received nine full scholarship offers from colleges and universities all over the United States; including one from Rutgers University, a few miles from home. I sat down and discussed options with Jane. She said follow your heart. At the time, I had no idea what that meant. I thought it meant to stay close to the ones you love. Jane was the only person who had taken good care of me after my parents' death. I had no real memory of my parents beyond a photo album I'd carried with me from foster home to foster home.   I decided to stay local and attend Rutgers. Jane laughed and asked why would you trade studying at Harvard with staying here; or not want to learn at Pepperdine located on the beach in Malibu? I told her the truth. My place was here. The world would wait for me to get my degree.

"Rutgers was a great school with its own literary press, and active social movement. Plus, it couldn't hurt that it was close enough to New York City for me to soak up all the international culture I could stand. Finally, Jane supported my decision and I accepted the scholarship to attend Rutgers in the Fall. She did put her foot down and demand I stay on campus though so I would learn how to be around anyone, respect diversity and be tolerant of others. I hadn't seen that one coming. I knew better than to push my luck, so I agreed. They had numerous campuses all over the state, and I picked to live on the campus two miles from the house. Again, Jane laughed and said, 'why defer life to stay home my dear Olivia!'

"I responded that life is lived where one locates themselves, not in searching for something out there beyond where you are. Searching is an illusion of what might be! I am under no illusion. People have to discover for themselves that wherever one goes, one is always there. The journey, well lived is the ultimate accomplishment no matter where one is. Jane nodded her head in affirmation and said, 'Brilliant point, well done!'"

She watched Javier's expression. She hoped he understood her meaning. It didn't really matter though. He didn't need to understand her. He wasn't going to be around long.

She launched into her least favorite part of her past.

"About six weeks before graduation, my teacher handed me a letter from the RWA chapter about the book. I opened it right there in the school hallway. It said I'd won the contest! The prize money was $5,000; my book was going to be featured in their chapter's newsletter and presented at the national convention in July in Orlando, Florida. I was in shock. I couldn't tell Jane yet, and it was still so very exciting. I thought maybe Jane and I could go to the conference together. I'd saved enough money to pay for the trip and since she loved reading romance novels, she could be amongst its elite writers.

"I still remember that day. I floated home on cloud nine. When I walked in the door, Jane was sitting in her favorite reclining chair. She'd been crying. I'd never seen her cry in the ten years I'd been there.

"What's wrong?" I asked and totally forgot about my excitement and elation.

"It's nothing." She said barely above a whisper.

"It's not nothing. You, my fierce mother, don't ever cry. So something has to be wrong!"

Jane looked at me. I saw a flicker of emotion and then a look of resignation. "You are a grown woman now, my Olivia, beautiful, feisty, strong and loving. You deserve the truth. As my role model, I will now emulate you and have the courage to be fierce as you say I am."

"I had such trepidation for what she was about to disclose. And yet, I too was courageous and determined to survive any words she might utter.

I said "no matter what, I can take it. I promise."

"I have cancer."

"Those three words. Words that instantly altered life. I didn't know what to say. I was never one to be at a loss for words. Jane took my silence as her opportunity to continue speaking.

"They said it's at an advanced stage. There is nothing they can do. I will likely die within three months."

"What? That can't be right. They're wrong. They don't know you. We'll fight it."

"No!" Jane said in a commanding voice that shook me. "I am not spending the last days of my life in a hospital fighting with no opportunity to enjoy what's left."

"Jane never raised her voice to me or anyone. Even when angry, she spoke softly. Now in this moment, she was clear and loud. The first tear slid down my cheek. It was the beginning of what seemed to be a dam welling up inside me. "Please, I pleaded with her. We cannot give up! I'm not ready for you to go."

"Oh child of mine. You misunderstand. I am not giving up. I am accepting the way of life."

"What do you mean?"

"We are all born to die. When it is our time to go, it's our time. While I might not be ready to die, nor you ready to let me go, the time is coming and we should prepare. We have a graduation and your future to celebrate a short time from now. I will be there, you have my word. Now, let's brighten our subject. How was your day?"

"Just like that Jane had dropped that topic and picked up a new one! I too let it go in hopes the doctors had gotten it wrong and I had many more years of life left with my mother Jane. It was time to prepare for Jane's last days, however long that might be.

"Shortly after Jane's announcement, I was selected as senior class valedictorian as I had the highest grade point average. Jane was noticeably getting sicker. I didn't want to speak at graduation. I wanted to cry, hide and stay in the house. Jane said 'this honor of speaking to your fellow classmates is not about you. It is about others you might inspire along the way. Leave them fully living life, as precious as we now know it to be. Share with them what you told me about living life fully now, right here where we are.' She went on to conclude by saying 'the choice is up to you; yet I compel you— you must go make a difference!'

"On graduation day, when I gave my speech, I suppressed the tears that threatened every time I looked over to Jane. She looked so frail, yet determined. She'd needed a nurse to accompany us to the ceremony, and she was a proud mama! When I walked across the stage and received my diploma, I knew I had accomplished something beyond words. I had given myself permission to be happy, to be loved, to give of myself and to receive from others. That was a victory for the wimpy child I'd once been.

"Jane was to return back home shortly after graduation was over. She'd compelled me to stay for the reception that followed the ceremony, and I'd refused. Two could be stubborn. I learned from the best. Home we went.

The nurse and I helped Jane into bed, and she looked about ready to pass out. In my graduation robe, I made and served our tea party. Jane gave me a basket full of gifts, including a rare edition of Jane Austen's book *Pride and Prejudice*. And then I presented my gift to her—my first published book. I'd had a book cover designed to include a Victorian mansion, and entitled it Jane's Cottage. I didn't tell her about the planned trip we would've taken if she had been well, as I knew she'd be disappointed.

"She asked I read it to her, including the directions to me: 'don't skip any of the salacious parts.' I laughed out loud. What did I know of grown people's love stories? I'd barely been kissed by a fumbling teenage boy in the neighborhood. I used the books I'd read as a guide in my writing. I certainly never planned to read it to my mother. Life is hysterically funny at times with its ironies.

Over the next few days, I read the novel to Jane. When we came to the end, with tears in her eyes, she said, 'what a beautiful love story! Thank you again for sharing yourself with me. Publish it! Promise me, you will continue to be a force to be reckoned with in this world. Also, promise me you will keep writing these love stories throughout your life. Love passionately and hold nothing back. Read them to your husband, children and grandchildren.'

I could deny Jane nothing, as she had given so much. I replied, "Yes ma'am."

A week later, Jane passed away in her sleep. I had been right there with her, reading one of my favorite Jane Austen books, *Sense and Sensibility*. When she'd stopped her labored breathing, I knew she'd left me. I cried my heart out. I screamed as I'd hugged her one final time. I remember saying, Death, why does this keep happening to me, losing my parents and leaving me alone. There was no response.

Javier spoke. "What in heaven did you do?"

"I got it together though when I stopped feeling sorry for myself. Jane had taken me in as a wounded little girl, and under her care she empowered and enabled me to have a life! The words in my speech from graduation, I shared at Jane's Irish wake/funeral celebration. I wasn't sad that day. I was determined to give a fitting tribute to the life and times of only mother I'd ever known. So with her friends and mine, we partied into the wee hours of the night. Jane would have been happy at her party. She was actually there in spirit, I know it. She lives in me always. I finally realized I had followed my heart right to Jane...and so I made good on my promise to her. I became a romance writer."

"Talk about an impressive story! Thank you for sharing it. You overcame great obstacles, I am sure you have only shared a small portion with me. I would one day like to read that novel."

"You are just being nice now. Men don't read romance novels. Don't pity me because of my story."

"I promise you, querida, I don't pity you at all. You are that beautiful, feisty, strong and loving woman your mother said you are."

"Thank you." Olivia said quietly as she turned to look out at the ocean. She sighed as she thought through his words. And she gave in, "yes, I will claim that."

"I would add in my own adjectives, but I will save them for another time, perhaps...now is the time for me to catch up on my sleep here next to you; for you to soak up the sun rays and write. Deal?"

"Deal!" Olivia said. *You sure do make a lot of deals with this man!* She needed some time to gather herself together.

Javier went from leaning on his right hand supported by his elbow and staring up at her, to lying face down on his stomach. It gave Olivia too much of a view. Instead of staring at him, as tempting as it was, she picked up her laptop and started to write again. It is a beautiful day and I am an author...

Chapter 6

"They slipped briskly into an intimacy from which they never recovered."
~ F. Scott Fitzgerald

Javier had been napping for a couple of hours and Olivia had ended up tilting the umbrella a while back so they both had shade. He'd not reapplied sunscreen before falling asleep. And while he unnerved her, she wasn't going to let him get burned to a crisp just to prove a point. Plus, he had been kind when he'd listened to her story without pitying her. She'd most especially appreciated that he didn't ask any more questions, didn't get sentimental and had decided to take a nap. They both knew in the silence they were letting the subject die.

"M'lady, I brought you a new drink." The waiter said.

"Thank you!" Olivia said as she turned sideways to sign for the newest fruity cocktail. Once that was done she reached out and took it from the server's tray. "It looks delicious."

"Yes, m'lady. It is a personal favorite of mine. Do enjoy!"

"I will and cheers" she smiled and bowed her head in gratitude.

"I see I have competition," Javier spoke from the lounge chair where he'd slept.

His voice had startled her and she almost dropped her drink. She noticed the server move away in a hurry all of a sudden. Her back was been turned to Javier. He must have just awakened from a deep sleep because she'd been watching him breathe before the waiter had arrived with the drink. She had hoped the quiet exchange would not have awakened the sleeping giant. But it had. Olivia took a sip, gathered some courage and set the drink on the table, then turned to face him. She smiled at the now sitting figure with a body that rippled in all the right places. She cleared her throat. "Why would you say you have competition and for what?"

"The waiter brought you a fresh drink. He is interested in you, not in serving me."

"Oh, he can't be interested in me. They know I tip well, and I made arrangements hours ago to keep the drinks coming so I'd stay happy and hydrated. I did ask if you wanted a drink and you declined."

"Bella, I bet he is all too willing to keep you plied with liquor."

"I'm fine. As I've told you before, I can take care of myself. Anyway, how was your nap?"

"Refreshing. But now I am thirsty. May I have some?" he said as he pointed to her cup sitting on the table where she'd left it.

"Ummmm, okay, sure." She reached over, picked up the cup and gingerly handed it to him. She was actually tired of drinking liquor anyway and needed to consume the rest of her water. Water would offset the effects of the alcohol on her almost empty stomach.

He took a sip and then poured it out onto the sand next to him. "Just as I thought. This drink is an island concoction the natives consume. It turns one into a wild party animal, easy to be taken advantage of: robbed, raped, kidnapped or the like."

"Why'd you pour it out? What do you mean? The wait staff is trying to make me intoxicated? Is it not safe to be a tourist here?"

"At times it is safe. The waiters like to get the foreign women drunk. Then when the hot alcohol is in your system, you will parade around, be loose with your money and your body."

"Why would they do that?"

"In your instance, I'm not sure. Clearly they see I'm here, so no harm will come to you. You are not naive Olivia. These games play out between men and women all over the world. I could not in good conscience allow you to drink it. I'll owe you a drink. No matter to concern yourself further, I know the bar owner. I will speak with him and let him know what's going on."

"Thanks, I think! I cannot believe people can be so cruel in such a beautiful paradise."

He shrugged as if it was no big deal. "Everyone has their own agenda, some are more honorable than others. Anyway, are you about ready to go?"

"Yes, why?"

"Let's go for a stroll on the beach. If we walk in that direction," he pointed down the beach and her eyes followed, "it is on the way to our resort and it takes us along the western shore."

"I suppose that would be the okay." She closed her laptop and pushed it into her beach bag. Then gathered her little bit of stuff and also put it in her bag.

Javier got off the lounger and reached out his hand to help her up. Olivia placed her hand in his. Once on her feet she swayed slightly. She was a little light-headed. Javier noticed too as he put his left hand on her hip to steady her. "Are you okay?"

"Yes, I think so."

"Okay, let me get your stuff."

He reached down and grabbed her beach dress. He held it so she could slide her arms into the sleeves, then wrapped it around her body, and tied the belt in a loose knot around her waist. She didn't like being dressed by someone else but she was thankful for his assistance. She looked up into his darkened eyes. "Thank you! I'm hungry."

She was going to have lunch when she got back to the hotel. The snacks she'd tucked away were a long ago memory, and her intoxication lurked behind the scenes. It was probably a good thing he had happened along to invade her escape. Who knew what was really in that last drink or what would have occurred if she'd finished it.

"Me too," he said.

As he looked down into her eyes. She swayed just a little bit. Was he talking about hungry for food or her. It would be so easy to kiss him right now, she thought. But no, she didn't want the effects of the liquor to be an excuse. When she kissed him, if she kissed him, she wanted to have a clear mind.

"Okay, let's head back to civilization and food!"

He picked up her bag and carried it for her. They started a slow stroll back to the grounds of their resort.

A little ways down, the Pilot chose a paved path that took them along a shady grove overlooking the ocean. Both of them were quiet, enjoying the serenity of the beach and lapping waves in the distance. The birds hopped along looking for prey, and the bugs were content to flutter around pollinating the blooming flowers.

With each step, Olivia was sobering and becoming more aware of the man next to her. She had never been in paradise in the company of a man. Even though she and Javier were not touching, the scene seemed so private, almost intimate. They were passing a group of trees with a swing hanging from one of the big branches.

"That is beautiful" she said. "I wonder what it's like to swing back and forth as one watches nature's beauty unfold."

"Would you like to swing and find out?"

She stopped in the middle of the path. "No, no. I am dizzy. I am already embarrassed enough. I don't think falling on my face is a good idea too."

"A pity. Well I will owe you a swing ride for another time, si?"

"Si! I just might take you up on your offer once I am clearheaded again!" They kept walking and continued their comfortable silence.

Before long they had arrived back at their resort.

Olivia spoke first. "Oh we've made it back. I appreciate you making sure I got here safe and sound."

"My pleasure. Have lunch with me?"

"No thank you. Rain check please? I am going to order room service and take a nap."

"Very well. Enjoy your meal and nap." He handed forward her bag and Olivia took it. He turned to go.

"Javier..."

"Si querida," he said turning back to face her. "Did you change your mind?"

"No!" she said firmly. "I just wanted to tell you, I really did have a good time with you at the beach."

"So did I querida. I'll check on you later."

"Okay." She watched him turn and walk in the direction of the buffet restaurant. Olivia's stomach growled just then. Right, feed yourself! Olivia sighed and turned in the direction of her room.

******

Hours had past and the sun was setting. From her oceanfront suite, Olivia could see the last of its rays casting light on the dark shadows of the water. The iridescent shimmer welcoming the sun to disappear under the horizon.

Paradise was going to sleep, or so was the pretense. Olivia knew better. With sunset, the partying always continued in paradise, every day of the week. Music, drinking and dancing would be the flavors of choice. Hot steamy nights of passion would play out and lead the way for people to fulfill on fantasies or cause nightmares. The players in the game would perform their lines and feign ignorance to the outcomes. Happiness or heartbreak...love or hate...there is no middle ground. *Olivia, stop! You are sounding like a sad poet! Plus, you can't keep living your life from what happened with John. Hell, you never even went to paradise with him.*

Right! Olivia said as she sat parked in front of the living room's balcony window where she continued to reflect back on her day. Matter of fact, she'd thought of little else since her much needed shower, lunch and a nap.

It was dinner time and she wasn't even interested in food. She didn't dare go back out. She knew if she did it was with only one intention in mind—to be on a quest to find the Pilot. The resort wasn't big enough to keep their paths from crossing. What would she say to him? What would she do? She was so ready to kiss his lips, to run her hands over the planes of his naked, muscled flesh. Oh stop Olivia! Let's keep this politically correct before you get more hot and bothered.

She realized Javier had been great company today and his sense of duty to watch over her was surprisingly inviting. Olivia wondered if he'd have that same level of care if he made love to her. Most men were only interested in their pleasure and release. Javier seemed genuinely interested in her well-being. She could even tell he was physically attracted to her. Yet, he wasn't offering her anything and he didn't force her to go beyond simple chatter. He could've taken advantage of her with that drink in her system. And he didn't. One for sure fact is she had an intense desire to 'get physical' with him. She couldn't be certain her lust for him wasn't related to the effects of the crazy drink not yet out of her bloodstream. Except that she'd had the same fantasies sober too. Olivia sighed. Her inner voice chimed up: *what are you gonna do missy?*

As if on cue with an answer, the phone rang on the desk.

She jumped up and answered. "Hello!"

"Good evening querida. I was calling to see how you're feeling."

"Javier?" she said even though she knew damned well it was him.

"Si, it is I. How are you?"

"I'm good. Just been taking it easy since I got back to my room. How are you?"

"I'm great. I have been a little worried about you."

"Why? I wasn't that intoxicated. The effects are gone and I had a perfect respite. Please, really don't worry about me."

"I suppose it is the way we were raised. Mama droned into us to always be a gentleman and look after others. I'm glad to hear all is well. Any interest in having dinner with me?"

"Thank you for the offer, and I think I'm going to just stay in tonight. I'm don't really want any more food today."

"A rain check then perhaps? I have a few days off so I'll be around."

"Yes, a rain check when I have an appetite and you're paying."

He chuckled. "My pleasure! Sweet dreams querida."

"Goodnight Javier, and thanks for calling to check on me." She hung up the phone before she changed her mind.

What? Another night alone? Just lovely! This isn't seeming like paradise. You're going to spend hours thinking about him when you could be with him. What sense does that make? It's the best move she said out loud. I am not thinking straight. I am not inviting trouble into my life tonight, not even for his offer of a free dinner.

Chapter 7

"The most eloquent silence; that of two mouths meeting in a kiss."
~ Anonymous

It had been a good day so far, thought Olivia, barefoot and lounging across her bed reading about what else Barbados had to offer in the way of romantic settings. All was quiet. It was after five in the afternoon and she was contemplating a little siesta. The joys of being self-employed with no exact schedule meant one could take a siesta whenever the mood hit. As her eyes started to close, she thought she heard a knock on the door. Jumping up and padding across the soft, plush beige carpet, she looked through the peephole. A familiar vision was standing there. Pasting a smile on her face that she did not feel, she opened the door. "Javier, what do you want?"

"Olivia, I want to talk. We must talk!"

"Really, a man who actually wants to talk! Are you feeling okay?"

"Si. Yes. Look there is this intense attraction we have for each other. I get we said that it would be foolish to just fall into bed with each other. It is like a fire that burns when we are in the same room together. Surely you must feel it."

She sighed. "Yes, I feel it. So what? There are plenty of times when I have been attracted to men and not acted on it. So as I was saying, what do you want?"

He stepped forward into the room. "Olivia, please talk to me. I want you. I dream about you. I want to know what it is like to feel you in my arms. For two days and nights I have wondered, and I can't take much more."

She took a tentative step forward. With the same sleep deprived nights, she had dreamt of a moment when he might show up and make love to her. She was unsure if it was a good idea to act on what she felt with him. After all, she did not know Javier from Adam and he had the power to burn her with a look, a brief touch. That was not a good sign. He could be an international playboy, a married man, or worse. Who knows! Yet, she had yearned for him to hold her since she met him two days ago. In big, strong arms she was meant to cling. Get a grip, Olivia she said to herself. You are starting to sound like a character in your own romance novels. He impatiently stood there.

As she shifted the weight from one foot to the other, she thought to herself, there is no harm in talking, right? Javier did not seem like the patient type. With that set of facts it did seem inevitable that they would have to come to some conclusion. Moving aside to let him pass all the way into her suite, she exhaled. "Okay Javier, come in and let's talk." She went back into the bedroom to her queen-sized bed near the window and sat down on the edge. It did not make sense to sit in the living room chairs. If they were going to discuss sex, might as well get to the point. She was not inviting him to sit on her bed. She pointed to the other bed for him to sit. So he sat on the corner opposite her. Dressed in black jeans and a form fitting tan t-shirt, he looked the epitome of calm, cool and collected. Oh yeah, and as sexy as any man she had the pleasure to sit across from in any bedroom. Hey she thought, that might be a good line to put into my next book.

Bringing her attention back to him, she searched his face. "Talk!" she said and stared at his lips awaiting whatever illogical thing he planned to say to make her give in.

"Olivia, first of all thank you for letting me in. I hope you trust me. I would never intentionally upset you or bring you any harm. I must tell you, I have never had a woman get to me like you are getting to me. Every time I close my eyes, I think of you. I want to kiss you, hold you, make love to you. I am shy too, especially when I really like someone. You may not realize but I do not often do this. Women are always around me, and so what! Not to say that I am a virgin." And lifting his eyebrow above his left eye, he said "tell me you are not either? Never mind. I don't want to avoid dealing with this, with us. I want to give you every pleasure. I have nothing to offer you and yet, I still want you." He drove his hand through his dark curls. "Ugh, I am not saying this right. Hell, I don't know how to do this." He lay back on that queen-sized bed and covered his head with a pillow.

Olivia was enthralled with the frustration and sincerity all wrapped up into this handsome man. She did not know what to do either. He took up the whole bed with his body and it was a very nice body to stare upon from afar. She could perhaps stare at him for hours studying every inch of his muscular physique. On feeble legs, and yet drawn to him she went over to the bed, climbed up onto her knees and met him in the center of the bed. She moved the pillow away from his face so she could see into his eyes. It was like she was on auto-pilot and she certainly did not have a license.

"Javier, you are irresistible." He awakened a passion that she had never known and that was all before he had even kissed her. "One thing is for sure," she continued, "I am not a virgin. I may not have as much experience as you. I don't know whether this will create a regret for either of us, and here I am."

It was a moment in which she did not know what to do. She ran her right leg over the left one and felt the softness of her skin. It left her longing for what could be if she allowed it. He was the one who imagined how this would all play out. It was a sexy dream that took place on the beach with both of them living out their dreams. Somebody was going to have to be willing to take the risk, be vulnerable, and give their heart.

Patience, someone once said, is a virtue. She never considered herself a virtuous woman so now what?

With a long sigh, she said, "Javier, make love to me." He leaned up and she lowered her head. Their lips met in a kiss. Soft, gentle and controlled. She sighed aloud. "Mmmm." As she leaned into his body, she pushed all the pillows aside so there was nothing to get in the way. He reached up and put his hand against her cheek. He deepened the kiss, his tongue reaching out to duel with hers. She could not think, nor did she want to think. All Olivia knew was she had now, and if only for one night as the song says, then so be it. They shifted on the bed and she ended up pressed against his body as if fitting herself to the dimensions of his muscled chest and strong legs. He pulled her up on top of him. "Good," she said smiling down into his eyes, "I like being on top!"

"Si Bella, I like having you on top of me," his throaty voice said. "You fit so perfectly in my arms, are so enticing, such a siren of seduction." He kissed her again on her mouth. Then with his tongue he placed wet kisses on her face, kissing her right ear lobe and then her left. She was so turned on…nothing good could come from being this attracted to a man. Who cares, now is all we ever have. She made a silent promise to love every moment, to sear each moment into her memory bank to carry with her when she walked away from him.

He pushed up her shirt trailing his hands up her back. He took her breasts in his hands and caressed them. Achieving his desired result with her shirt up, he leaned her over to the side and bent his head. Then kissing her right nipple. She wanted more, needed more. He whispered "my goodness Olivia, you are beautiful. Your breasts are beautiful."

She felt herself rubbing her body against his, melding herself to him as if she could not get close enough. She could not remember the last time she felt this much passion, if ever. She moaned into his neck. "This feels so good."

"Olivia, is this what you want? You want me?"

"Yes, I want this. I want you…why fight it."

"I want to feel your skin against mine." She sat up and took her shirt off. She pulled on his shirt wanting all of him. Half-naked, she smiled. "I'm hot now."

"Yes you are." He flipped them over so she was now on the bottom and stole a quick kiss. He sat up, took off all his clothes and pulled off the rest of hers. He stood above her fully naked. Her eyes met the mischief in his eyes. Unable to resist seeing the rest of him as the late day sunlight placed a soft glow around the scene. His skin was so smooth and her eyes slowly moved downward. All she wanted was to feel his naked body on hers, in her, and bringing her pure ecstasy. Climbing on the bed in slow motion he pushed his body up toward her lips. He lay on top of her, his body against hers, and reached for her hands that were above her head. Weaving his fingers through hers, he kissed her in a passionate lip lock. They held hands and then just that quickly, the hand holding ended as did that kiss.

Javier thought to himself, so many other places to kiss…from her lips, to her cheeks, her breasts and onward. Never one to waste an opportunity to have it all, he left her breasts alone, and held her body in his hands. He made a trail of kisses down her body. Her belly button…Javier, trying not to come prematurely, began to kiss more of her. She smelled of a blend of pure womanhood and a soft flowery scent he could not exactly place. Maybe it was rose, gardenia, or jasmine. Definitely a musk mixed in that was intoxicating. His mom favored floral scents—he pushed that thought aside as his mom was not the visual he wanted right now.

Just then, he lowered his lips to kiss the apex of her womanhood. He stuck out his tongue and licked her. She moaned and came up off the bed. Once was not enough. Standing up on the floor, he pulled her legs toward him, and pushed her knees apart. He squatted down, placed himself between her legs, and went about his duty to bring her immense pleasure. He might not have much to offer her other than sex, and this was one area he was an expert. He wondered how many times he could make her orgasm. She was moaning in the softest

97

way. He thought he felt her spasms begin. Her hands reached out and held his head to her. She was wiggling. Of course that was just an invitation for him to keep going. Exactly how sensitive was she? He was going to make this memorable, give her as many orgasms as she could stand. And then he was going to be inside her, moving in a dance between a man and woman that was as old as time. A few minutes later, he could feel her spasms starting and she tried to pull back. He held her to him in a tight grip. Her noises getting louder and louder until she shuttered. He licked her up and down.

Olivia was about undone. After exquisite orgasm number two, Olivia was in pure ecstasy. She could keep having orgasms, and yet it was not enough. She reached down and pulled Javier up to her.

"What's wrong?" He whispered.

"Absolutely nothing! That was amazing. And now it's your turn." He kissed her. She got to taste her essence on his lips. What a turn on. She pushed him onto his back, and trailed kisses down his body. She reached out and held his manhood in her hands. His erection was hard and she could not help kissing him, tasting him, caressing him, stroking him, and giving him the same pleasure he had given her. More than anything she wanted him moving inside her. All in due time. Just when she was sure she was about to make him come, he reached out and pulled her back up to kiss her.

"I want to be inside you – NOW. I need to find my pants to get a condom to protect you."

"Do you have any diseases I should know about?"

"No and I regularly get checked."

"I do not have any either, and I'm on the birth control pill."

"What are you saying Olivia?"

"I'm safe. We're safe, no need to get a condom." She then straddled him and reached out to guide him inside her. Once they had joined all she could think was oh my! It felt good to finally get him inside the hot warmth of her body. She began to move up and down; they picked up the pace faster and faster until she could not hold back the orgasm. She let go and came for the third time. This could be addictive she thought to herself.

"Will you be on top?"

"You, Bella mia, want me be on top?"

"Yes, it seems only fair that I should share the wealth."

"Of course, your wish is my command."

"Don't come out" she said. He flipped her to the right on her back. Just then he slipped out of her and she realized how wet they were. "We are soooo wet!"

"Yes, no kidding, we are. I think we will get even more wet."

"You feel so good inside me." He pushed inside her again and started to move in a slow pace that became faster and faster. Moments later as she held onto him with all she had, she felt another explosion that left them both clinging to the other. "Yes, just like that...don't stop." They came together in a heated exchange.

A few moments later when it seemed the spasms had calmed, Javier lifted himself off her, and pulled her body close to his. Almost immediately he missed her body surrounding him. He leaned over and gently kissed her on the mouth. She was amazing. With his fingers he trailed circles on her breasts and stomach. Oh my, he could spend all day and night sucking on her beautiful breasts. And he was so turned on. Not sure if one time would ever be enough. Would it satisfy his curiosity? If he could satiate himself of her, then he could move on. It was never healthy to want something more than rational behavior. They laid in bed just holding each other for quite some time. He wanted to stay. That was not like him. He needed to leave her, go back to his room, and sort himself out. He kissed her forehead and got up from her side. She half-heartedly watched him get dressed. "What will you do now?"

Olivia stopped staring at him and looked over to the clock on the wall. It was half past seven in the evening. "I will likely take a shower, eat and go to bed."

It was going to be awkward between them, she could sense it already happening. What could she say—she gave in and had sex with him, she satisfied her desires. She was grateful it had happened finally, so she did not go crazy. She could not tell him that. What did one say...maybe nothing was best.

He said "thank you for an amazing time."

"Ditto," she said.

He smiled, one of those irresistible smiles that made her weak. "Goodnight love...I will see you in the morning. And then we will talk about this. Agreed?"

"Yes, agreed." She said half sleepy and not sure what she was agreeing to.

As if in slow motion, he leaned over and gave her a way too passionate kiss goodnight. She stayed laying in the bed as he left her room. In that moment, she realized they sealed the deal with each other. It was wonderful and amazing. When he was gone, she dragged herself from the bed and locked the door.

Into the shower she went, feeling tender in areas that she had forgotten could be tender. It was a great time and it was over. She thought that once would be enough; one time with no strings attached. Beside herself, she relived her memories, wiped away the lonely tear. Despite her best efforts, he had gotten in under her defenses.

When the shower was over, she dried off and put on the terry cloth robe. She found a granola bar in her bag and munched it all down. She was not going outside. She needed some sleep. She picked up her discarded clothes and tossed them on a chair. Then she checked the door lock, and flipped the do not disturb sign outside on the door knob and relocked herself in. She climbed into bed, exhausted, satisfied and glad he'd left her to pick up the pieces. Tomorrow she would put the façade back in place. She might not want to forget the memory. Still life goes on and Javier did not fit into her world. She would push him out.

Chapter 8

"True love is not a hide and seek game: in true love, both lovers seek each other." ~ Michael Bassey Johnson

The next morning, Olivia awoke to the sound of her alarm going off. She had forgotten to turn it off. She had fallen asleep soon after her shower had ended last night. While she lay there reliving the moments of passion with Javier, she was also lamenting that they had slept together. Sex complicated everything. Why, because she was incapable of taking it for what it was— one night, a weak moment.

She heard a knock at the door. Was this déjà vu? She hoped it was him. Did she? After last night, the first time they had made love. Correction, had sex, she was not sure whether either of them had made the right decision. She hadn't slept much. Nothing new there as she had not slept much since she'd met him. When the sun had risen over the ocean and she was still awake, all she had was a body tender from his total control and a lot of confusing thoughts. She was not the kind of woman to have a fling or an affair in paradise. Yet she reminded herself again, that is all this could be. It was one night, a brief encounter. She heard the knock again. It had to be him. She got out of the bed, put on the terry cloth robe that laid across the bottom of the bed. When he left last night, she had placed the Do Not Disturb tag on the door. It was too early in the morning for the maid to ignore the request and no other guests would be so bold as to continue to knock on the door.

103

She just opened it without looking out. And as she stared into his composed, calm face, she confirmed it was the Pilot in the flesh. He looked her up and down, and as if approving purred "Good Morning Olivia. Why are you opening the door without knowing who is at the door. I do not like it. Please always look as you are a woman, traveling alone. You never know who might be on the other side of the door."

"Hello, Javier, is it a good morning? Did you not see my Do Not Disturb sign on the door."

"But of course Bella. I figured it was my invitation to visit. How did you sleep?"

"I have not slept much," she admitted.

Looking concerned, he pulled her into his arms and tilted her head up so he was looking directly into her eyes. His look was searching. "Why not? Are you sick? Was it because of what happened with us last night? Are you regretting making love with me?"

"Javier, it is not like I wanted to be disturbed by anyone. Since you ignored that, please do come in. I do not want to broadcast what we did last night to all my neighbors."

"Very well." He pushed her back into the room so that she was no longer holding the door open. As soon as the door shut, he spun her around and gently pushed her back against the closed door. There was no doubt in her mind that he was aroused as his erection pressed against her stomach through her terry cloth robe. Her hands were down at her side and he rested his on the door. "Now, my querida, you were telling me why you did not sleep much."

"Was I?"

"Si, please tell me."

Ignoring his request, she asked, "Javier, why are you here?"

"As promised, I am here to talk about what is happening with us. Also, I wanted to know if you would have breakfast with me and then perhaps we could go swimming. It seems wasteful to eat alone when we have this connection between us." Smiling, he added "and I am sure we could both use some exercise. What do you think?"

"I think I do not want breakfast or a swim. I just want to lounge around this morning and get some rest."

"Such a shame. If you want, I would be willing to lounge around and rest with you."

"I do not think that is such a good idea. What happened last night was amazing. And it was a one off."

"That would be such a tragedy querida. I enjoyed myself and I want you again. I think you want me again too. I can feel your body getting hot here pressed against mine."

"That might be true, and I am not the kind of woman to engage in brief affairs. We are both adults so let's not kid ourselves. It was good sex."

"Were you just using me for research on your book?"

"No! I do not use people. I am grown with no regrets. And I am not some trophy or prize so I do not treat others as such. One more thing, I am not mistress material. Now I need to pretend I do not like you, am not attracted to you. I am."

"Yes, Olivia, please do not think I have a label for you. All I know is we have this connection. I thought one time would be enough, a one off, as you said. This morning when I awoke, I wanted to see you."

"That is very flattering, and what happened between us was crazy." She bit her lower lip as if pondering her next words. "And it was good too."

"Yes it was." He leaned in and kissed her forehead. "I will leave you to get some rest. Let me know if you change your mind. I mean about a meal and swim. While I want you, as is evident, I want you to want me with no regrets."

"Thank you for understanding."

He leaned over and gave her a passionate kiss on the lips. A kiss that left her breathless and longing for more.

"Why did you kiss me?"

"I like kissing you. Other than right now, I cannot give you anything. Don't fall for me, and yet I want you to want me. You see, Olivia, you are special. There is something about you unlike any other woman I have ever met. You challenge me to think, and you gave all of yourself to me last night—a man you do not know. You deserve a man who can take care of you, all your needs, contain your passions. I am not him. I will sleep with you, make you feel pleasure beyond anything you ever imagined, and I will walk away. You are someone a man could get lost in. I am not capable of loving you Olivia."

"Wow, I went from being special to you to your not being capable of loving me. There has to be a compliment mixed up in there somewhere."

"Oh, Bella mia what I said was meant to be a compliment."

Olivia liked a challenge. "There is something I should tell you. I get what I want. I cannot help it Javier, it has always been that way. If I choose to have you, I will. If I don't, I won't."

He said, "Oh really! Well this time you might lose with me."

"It is a chance I might have to take. Don't deny me what I want just because I told you that. Anyway, the jury is still out for me about you."

"We shall see; I make no promises other than right now. Keeps it simple."

"Javier, let's be clear, I did not ask you for anything. You do not owe me anything."

"Neither of us owe the other anything Olivia."

"For now, I'm tired and need some sleep."

"Si, querida. I will go now. Make no mistake though, I will be back."

"Perhaps after I get some sleep, I would like to have that meal."

He removed himself from her body taking a step back. "Excellent news. I will check on you later."

Immediately Olivia felt a chill from the loss of his body against hers. "Thank you again."

He simply smiled, reached to open the door. The Do Not Disturb sign fell to the floor. He reached down, picked it up, placed it back on the door knob and stepped into the hallway.

Just as quickly as he appeared, he was gone.

******

Later that afternoon, Olivia felt like a new woman. She had slept a few more hours, had a spa treatment, a relaxing soak in the spa Jacuzzi, and a lite lunch. She had stopped beating herself up for her choice to sleep with Javier. She was just settling into reading a magazine when the phone rang. She answered.

"Did you miss me Bella," he asked?

"Yes. And did you miss me?" she countered.

"Yes. Of course."

"Good. I want you inside me. Call me greedy. You feel good, and I want sex. I want you. I bet we are both really wet right now. Why don't you come over and show me how much you missed me?"

She heard his sharp intake of breath. "Be there in five minutes." And then the phone line went dead. Olivia looked at her watch. Five minutes and counting. She went to stand at the door. Wanting to fidget she decided to open the door and leaned against the door jam.

Not more than four minutes elapsed and she saw him coming down the hallway. There was a deep, intense look on his face. "Hi," he said.

She moved off the door. "Hi yourself" she said as she turned and walked into her suite.

"Bella mia, did you change your mind?"

She heard the door close behind her. She was so hot for him. She pulled her shirt over her head as she went toward the bedroom. Next went the bra, and then she unzipped her pants and let them fall to the floor.

"I like that you strip for me. Take it all off please," she heard him say in a jagged voice.

"Shhhhhhh" she said as she put her finger up to her lips. She was in no mood to talk or even think through the logic of her choice. Her actions were speaking volumes and he got the message loud and clear. She turned around and untied the last bit of material from her body, a red lace thong that was covering so little. It fell to the floor too. She pushed her hair over her shoulders. All that was left were the high heels that she thought complemented her sultry look. She wanted him to want her like no other. She wanted him to take all his clothes off for her. "Javier, take off your clothes."

In one quick move he pulled off his shirt. Then he unhooked the button and zipper on his jeans, and pushed them down his legs. Under them he was naked. As soon as her eyes refocused she could see his erection at her full attention.

She turned and walked the rest of the way to the bed. She laid on top of the covers and spread her legs for him as she leaned back. He was over there in what felt like two seconds.

"Woman, you are going to make me come before I even touch you." He climbed on top of her as he began to stroke his erection.

Olivia was in a state of pure arousal. She reached out and replaced her hand where his had been. "It's okay," she reassured him. "There is always another orgasm."

He kissed her and she could feel his arousal ready to slide into her. She pointed him toward the tip of her core. She knew she was all slick and wet and just begging to be satiated. She wiggled a little bit and he moved off her. She heard him say "wait, not yet."

"Wait?" Was he going to make her beg? She was ready to beg.

Instead he turned her on her side and he moved in next to her. Laying side by side spooning, he whispered into

111

her ear. "I want you." She reached her hand up to rub his face and into his hair. He pulled her back into him, stretched his hand down to her vagina and caressed her.

"Why are we waiting, Javier? We both know nothing will satisfy this except you inside me. You touching me is making me wetter."

He gave her a breathy chuckle. "Just my talking to you makes you wet."

"Good point."

"You know you love it."

"I do. Promise you will put me out of my misery soon."

"Si querida. I promise to make you come many, many times." He kissed her earlobe and she felt his wet tongue demanding her complete submission. At that moment, he pushed his finger inside her and she came off the bed to meet his touch. He rubbed her and pushed into her simultaneously. All the while he was whispering words she barely recognized into her ear. She was almost sure it was Spanish. She was so enthralled in the feeling that she could not concentrate, she didn't care what he was saying. As the pace picked up, her breathing increased as well. She let go into a free fall of spasms.

When she regained a little sanity, she pushed him onto his back and licked her lips. "Mmmm, now it's my turn to pleasure you." Slowly she kissed his lips, and then used her tongue to lick her way down his body. All she wanted to do was make him come just like he had made her fall apart. How could life feel this good. She did not know, and had no time to think. At that exact moment her lips met his erection, she was lost again in the moment of tasting him, loving him, and sending him over the edge so he felt her passion.

Javier spoke aloud, "I love making love with you. You are so responsive, so intense. You are going to make me come, and I want to be inside you before that happens."

She loved that he saw her as sexy and alluring. She was on top of him when she stopped her assault on his erection. He pulled her up to him as she glided her body slowly up his damp skin. Their mouths met in a passionate kiss. His tongue was inside her mouth, hers dueling with his. As if they were the perfect fit when joined together, he slid his erection into her vagina. The feeling was so good. Back and forth, up and down, from slow to fast. She let him guide her as he held onto her bottom. He was kissing her breasts, her neck. Everywhere his lips went, it intensified the belonging, their connection as they both headed over the cliff toward pure ecstasy.

She yelled out, "Javier, don't stop. Please don't let me go. This feels too good and I am going to come for you again." He was like a drug to her body. Unable to resist, they both let go and the pairing was complete. This is where she belongs, where they completed each other. Like a cat purring after being satiated with warm milk, and attention, she rolled over and sighed.

Everything would work out, of this she was sure. That was her last thought before she fell into a deep sleep on top of him.

Chapter 9

*"One ought to hold on to one's heart; for if one lets it go, one soon
loses control of the head too."*
~ Friedrich Nietzsche

Olivia opened her eyes and saw Javier, who she thought
would be asleep next to her under the covers, standing
on the other side of the room. He was putting on his
pants with his back towards her. He'd spent the night.
She remembered waking up a numerous times in the
night, making love and falling back to sleep wrapped in
his arms. It had been countless times, too many and yet
her need for him was fierce. "Morning," she said.

He turned around and walked back over to the bed and
sat down on the side where she lay. He ran a finger
down her cheek and said, "Morning Bella."

"Why are you dressed? Where are you going?"

"I need some coffee. I'm going to run downstairs, check
my messages, get some java and will be back shortly.
Do you want some or perhaps some hot tea?"

"Oh. Ummmm, yeah. Tea would be good" she said as
she yawned. "Something herbal please, with two sugars
and cream. Take the key off the table so I do not have to
get up to let you in."

"As you wish." He leaned over and kissed her gently on the lips. Then he rose from the bed and disappeared into the next room.

Olivia heard the suite door close. She rolled over in the bed, twisted in the covers. The sun was up and a new day had again dawned. She yawned. Time to get up. She rose from the bed, and went through to the bathroom intent to take a shower. She'd be fully dressed by the time he returned. She had spent more time in bed over these last few days, than she had in a long time. It was not a good look—she was not a good time girl. She was an educated woman, and she needed to gain some perspective. Being too attached and clingy with a man could be the downfall of a woman. He had already told her not to look for him for a future or anything beyond now. An affair in paradise could lead to heartbreak. He would leave, and where would she be? Everything was happening so fast. Could she do this? She was not sure anymore.

As she walked into the shower, she'd decided they needed to talk. When he got back, she would address this issue, even if it meant goodbye sooner rather than later.

******

When he returned an hour later, she was sitting on the living room sofa. She had been flipping through a magazine. In his right hand was a large take away cup.

116

"Your tea Senorita" he said as he placed it on the table next to her. "Herbal tea, with two sugars and cream as requested. Sorry it took me so long. I had more messages that I thought."

"Not a problem. It gave me a chance to get a shower and dress."

"I kind of hoped I'd find you still in the bed."

He leaned over and kissed her. He tasted like coffee and sugar. She moaned into his kiss and he kneeled down in front of her, while pushing her back. She wrapped her arms around his neck. All she wanted was to kiss him, feel him. It was like she was starved for him, the feel of his skin against hers. She realized there was little opportunity for skin to skin without removing some clothing. She started to pull at his shirt to release it from his jeans. She lifted her lips from his and whispered "you have on too many clothes."

"Your wish is my command, querida." He pulled back from her embrace and lifted his shirt over his head. Watching him was the biggest turn on. She followed his movements also pushing the shirt with her hands, desperate to touch his bare skin. She leaned down and kissed his chest. At the same time he began pulling her shirt off. He made quick work of that and tugged her pants down over her hips. He pulled her into his arms. "You feel so good in my arms." He leaned in and kissed her neck.

117

Damn she wanted him. Frustrated did not begin to describe what she was feeling. Yet, she knew if she did not stop him now, she would be lost again, and what would that resolve? "Javier, can we put this on hold for a couple minutes."

"Hmmm," he said between kisses. "Why do you want to put something this good on hold?" He kept on kissing her.

"Javier? Time out please."

He must have noticed she had a strange tone in her voice. He lifted his head to look at her. "Olivia, what's wrong?"

She pushed him back so she could stand next to the couch. "I need to tell you something."

He was frowning as he looked up at her. "What is it?"

"We really need to regain some control here. I am hot and bothered and cannot think."

He ran his hand through his hair. "Okay, I did get a little carried away. Sorry! Kissing you does that to me."

"Me too, as you can see from my state of undress."

"How about I go take a cold shower, you can take one if you want. Then we go get something to eat and discuss whatever is on your mind."

"As much as I want you, that sounds like an excellent idea. Go take your shower."

"Okay, right." He ran his hand through his hair again and then along his jawline. He rose from the floor, made a half turn and walked away and into the bathroom.

Olivia heard the shower turn on, and she exhaled. Until that moment, she did not recognize she had been holding her breath. She walked over to the mirror, and looked into her lustful stare. "Lawd, this man makes me lose all my control."

"Do I now?"

Olivia jumped. Had she really spoken out loud. Why did she keep getting herself into these messes. She allowed herself to look through the mirror at the almost naked Adonis man five feet away. After noticing his state of undress she meet his eyes. "I thought you went to take your shower."

"I did. I came to get my shaver from my caddy I brought back with me, and I heard you speaking aloud." He sat down on the sofa wrapped in a towel. "You know Olivia, I was thinking you could join me in the shower?"

She smiled. "I was just thinking that is not a good idea. If we get into the shower together, then we will end up in bed and nothing will get discussed."

He came to stand behind her. "Yeah, we do get carried away when we are this turned on."

She shifted around to face him. "You are right about that."

He reached out and pulled her into his arms. "Si querida, when I am near you, I want to touch you."

She could not resist running her hands through his curly hair.

He leaned over and kissed her neck, let his hands caress her back. His mouth found her right nipple and went to suck on it through her bra. In one quick moment he unclasped her bra. She left it fall to the floor as he licked her breast with his tongue.

"Javier," she said breathlessly, "what are you doing?"

"Olivia, you are beautiful. Please forgive me, I cannot resist you. I want you too badly." He pulled her back with him to the sofa as he sat down, putting her on his lap.

She kissed his forehead and straddled him. "I thought you were going to take a shower. Remember the water is running."

"Si." Rubbing against her with the towel coming apart was turning her into a wanton woman. She reached down to stroke his erection, finding him rock hard and ready for her.

Javier's lips consumed her in a mind-blowing kiss. She had to have him. Now. She pushed aside her hot pink thong and let his erection slide inside her. Being on top of him was one of her favorite places to be. She began to ride him as he sat on the couch. He helped glide her in and out. The pace was so frantic, so necessary as they chased the explosion that was worth every ounce of their strength. She could not resist. "Javier, you are making me come."

"Let go baby…when you let go, I will too."

They came together and slowly he laid back on the sofa as he held her in his arms. Her hair was a frantic mess of curls and sweat framing her face. He pushed the loose strands away as she lay atop him.

"You really are beautiful Olivia. I know you wanted to wait, to talk and I could not fight you, fight this."

"I am just as responsible for jumping on top of you." She eased out of his arms and stood up on weak legs. It was good. It is always good with you Javier. Now, go take your shower before I want more."

He got up, and kissed her forehead. "Ladies first. You go take your shower, while I look for my shaver. I promise to leave you alone for a few minutes. It will be a test of my will power."

Not long after they had both showered, they fell asleep in one another's arms on the bed. Waking to Javier's soft breathing against her neck, his arm possessively holding her in place, she quietly listened. There was something so special to Olivia about being held by this man. She was not sure what it was, and did not want to think too deeply or fool herself into making it mean anything at all. Their time together was good.

This moment was all that mattered. Talk was cheap, right?

"Penny for your thoughts?" she heard him mumble as if he could sense she was awake.

"Oh, I did not mean to wake you."

"You did not wake me," he whispered. "Our bodies are in tune with one another so I knew you were awake."

At that moment, Olivia noticed his erection also coming awake as it throbbed against her leg. Deep inside, she could feel her body already calling to him, begging him to pay attention to her, anticipating his possession as only he could take her over. A moment later her was on top of her, pushing deep inside her.

As he looked down into her eyes, he said, "One more time, and then I will be satisfied."

"Yeah, I will believe it when I see it."

"Are you complaining because I always want you?"

"No, not at all."

"Show me you want me, Olivia."

"If you would stop talking and let me focus, then I could show you."

******

Hours later, they were seated in the restaurant for brunch, all freshly dressed and basking in the afterglow of amazing sex.

"Okay Olivia, what did you want to talk to me about."

"I was just looking for a way to bring some sanity and control to what is happening between us."

He reached over and held her right hand. "What did you come up with Bella?"

"Not much. You see my attempts at bringing sanity, ended up with us back in bed."

He smiled, looking rather proud of himself. "Yes, I do. Is that so bad?"

She bit her bottom lip as she considered his question. "No, it has been amazing. Wonderful in fact."

"We said we would take it one moment at a time, right?"

"Yes, and this passion we have for one another, cannot be healthy."

"Well, not that I am complaining, but I am at a loss to solve it. Do let me know if you come up with a viable solution to extinguish our passion."

"I will. I mean, it will get resolved." Olivia was not convinced.

"Si, querida, it will."

They made small talk the rest of the meal. Olivia was hopeful the next moment would take care of itself. For now, she was content to enjoy her time with the Pilot.

Chapter 10

There was a knock at the door. Olivia was used to it now. She went to the door, looked through the peep hole and saw the Pilot there. She exhaled and pulled the door open. In swept Javier looking distracted. "Olivia, I must go. There is a serious storm looming and I must be there to help. Stay here! You do not have to leave Barbados as there is no threat to this island. Everything should be over in a week and I will come back here and see you."

"Well hello to you too!" she said as she closed the door. She'd heard his every word. Olivia was unsure why he needed to make plans for her. "I know I do not have to go. Remember, this is the place I chose to come for a few weeks. And in theory, I can come and go anywhere I want at any time. I am a grown woman! I earned the right over many years of staying put. And yet, if I stay here waiting for you, I will get more and more wrapped up in you. That does not seem like a healthy choice right now." Ah, the voice of reason. She turned from him and went to the balcony window to look out at the ocean.

He walked in, shut the door and came over to stand behind her. He did not reach out for her. However, if she stepped back a foot, she would be touching him.

"You are trying to hide your feelings from me? I thought we said we would deal with this head on."

She did not turn around. Instead, as she faced the ocean, she said "yes, well I did not expect to like you so much. I do not know what to do with it. It is not convenient for my carefree lifestyle."

"Querida, do you think it works any better for me?"

"Perhaps not, and you are a man. Men do not have those kind of feelings."

Mumbling under his breath, he ran his hand through his hair. "Look Olivia, I will not tell you how to feel and you do not tell me how to feel. Si?"

"Yes, deal, fine. I just want to go back to the way it was before we met."

Javier moved to stand directly in front of Olivia to block her from continuing to stare out the window. He lifted her chin with his hand, and looked deep into her blue eyes. "Impossible. We met. We have spent the last four days making love all over this hotel room. Do you think you will so easily forget? I won't. I do not want this to end."

"What now Javier? An illusion of a relationship that is not going to happen? You have to leave for work, and I am going to stay here, write and forget you."

"Really, my beautiful imp? You will not forget any more than I will." He leaned forward and placed the softest kiss at the base of her right shoulder, and then another a little lower down.

Almost giving in to seek out another kiss, she exhaled. "Javier, please stop. This is yet again another conversation that is going nowhere."

He lifted his head and straightened his body. She could see a seriousness had taken over where the playful demeanor had just been. "Answer me then please Olivia?" The unspoken arrogance and mischief in his dark eyes told Olivia that he was up to something. "Do you think you will so easily forget me?"

"No, I am sure it will take something for me to forget you. And my time here is paradise is not yet over so I will practice very hard to do just that."

Unconvinced by her statement, knowing the intensity of the passion and fire they ignited, he continued his assault to get his way. Just a little more time with her was all he wanted. Maybe not all, and he saw no point in having his thoughts go down that path right now. He had to convince her to not end this, them! "Do you have to stay here in Barbados?"

"You know that I do not."

"I have an idea."

"Oh, no…your ideas got me into your arms, your bed, and now I am a total mess. I am not used to this kind of wanton behavior."

"Ah, querida, I do not remember any serious complaints from you nor a lack of enthusiasm. Hear me out, por favor?"

"Okay fine. Just spit it out."

"I do have to return to work. How about I ensure you get to my private island which is only a thirty minute flight away. There you will find a great deal of peace and serenity in which to write. I even have internet. When I am done working, I will come to you and we can pick up where we left off. I dream of you on the beach, in my home. Come stay with me."

"That does not seem like a good idea Javier. You think it just so simple. First, it was stay here. Now it is come stay on my island. Incredible! You are all over the place, determined to have it go your way. What about what I want? Did you take that into consideration or do you just want to manipulate me?" Exasperated she did not know what to do. "There is a storm on the way! Will I be safe in your hut? And then do I look like the kind of girl who 'roughs it?' Your idea is ridiculous! I could not possibly come stay with you." Sensing herself weakening, she asked "I thought you worked away for weeks at a time? What sense does it make for me to stay there when you are not there."

She watched him smile as if he knew he was winning her over. "I do sometimes go away for weeks and it is close enough to here that I could work and have you too. I only stay in town when it becomes too unbearable to be alone at the beach. I do not live in a hut. It's an eight bedroom villa with amenities, a pool, on the beach and a staff willing to cater to your every need. I will be returning there anyway between shifts and I get quite lonely at times. With you there, it will be perfect. Think of the exquisite pleasure we could give each other day and night. I promise you will be safe. Just come and see. You are free to leave any time you want. You said work was flexible for you. You would have run of the house and the staff would tend to you when I am not there. I want you to want to go there and enjoy being with me. There are beautiful places where you could write, undisturbed."   .

"Javier, you are impossible!"light Already hearing her own voice soften to his desires, she faintly heard her voice utter, "what if I said I do not want to come and keep you company on your island, at your house, pool, beach, and have your staff cater to me?"   ˙

"I can easily tell the staff to leave the island."

"Ugh, that is not what I meant and you know it."

"Seriously, Olivia. The villa is just sitting there wasting away. Why spend the money to stay isolated here, when you could create a whole new experience for free. I promise you, I will see to your every need. It would be my pleasure to pamper you, feed you, bathe you, make love to you, devour you." He put his head on her shoulder. "You do not even have to sleep with me, if you don't want. You can have a suite of rooms for yourself and uninterrupted time to write. I know that is important to you." He captured her fingers between his and looked into her eyes with a stone serious look. "You are important to me, and I cannot yet let go of you. What do you think, Bonita?"

"You are important to me too Javier." Probably too important she mumbled to herself. "I will agree to come to your island. For one week. I promise you I will sort through this and figure out a way to get you out of my system. The sooner, the better."

"Deal…"

Chapter 11

"The ultimate goal of the architect...is to create a paradise. Every house, every product of architecture... should be a fruit of our endeavour to build an earthly paradise for people." ~ Alvar Aalto

The Pilot had deposited her here on his island earlier this afternoon with a quick, goodbye kiss and a brief introduction to Carmen and Pedro—his primary caretakers who lived in a cottage a few miles down the road. "I have to go. Please take good care of my woman," he'd said and ran back to his helicopter.

Carmen and Pedro had responded yes they would take care of me. Not that he'd stayed around to hear them utter the words. Within moments of his instruction, he left her side and ran back to the helipad. He took off as they all watched. She'd waved and then stood still like a mannequin until his helicopter disappeared somewhere off in the distance.

She thought to herself, did he really just leave me in the middle of nowhere? Wait, did he call me his woman? What have I gotten myself into...

"Here you are m'lady," Carmen said from behind her. "Welcome to our little island: Paradise Found, aptly named by Mr. Javier..."

Olivia turned and watched as Carmen curtsied and Pedro bowed.

"We are glad to have your company."

Then Olivia noticed the silver tray that held a hurricane glass filled a pretty blue liquid. It was accented with a turquoise and pink paper umbrella—the universal symbol of a tropical cocktail.

Where had that come from she wondered. Obviously, Carmen was very much adept at her job. She had been able to get the drink delivered in stealth mode. File for future reference. Olivia decided to keep those thoughts to herself.

She smiled and graciously accepted. "Thank you, what is it?" Olivia asked as she grabbed the drink and took her first sip. "Yum!"

"An island sparkle made of blue Curacao, lime, champagne and local rum," Carmen responded. "It reminds Mr. Javier of your eyes, which I do agree, are stunning."

Olivia blushed. "Thank you! But I don't understand? How would he have told you to make this for me?"

"Mr. Javier emailed ahead with his instructions. You will find he is quite thorough and organized about this place. He also said that you have free run of the villa, its facilities, and the island. You are to let us know if you need anything and it will be provided."

Javier hadn't bothered to tell her that or even consult with her. So controlling, that man! Best to bite her tongue and address it later to the source.

Seething inside, Olivia responded in a contrived happy tone, "Oh, I see. Well please don't go to any fuss on my account. I am no trouble at all." With a lift of the hand that held her drink, she went on, "this drink is refreshingly good and I am really appreciative."

"You're welcome Ms. Olivia," Carmen began. "It is our job to take care of things, act on Mr. Javier's behalf, and create an environment to host guests. That of course includes you. I put together a lite lunch for you. Should you need anything else before dinner, just ring."

"You are too kind."

"The pleasure is all mine."

"Ladies, please excuse me to go and finish watering the bougainvillea. I will first take your bag into the house. As my wife said, welcome Ms. Olivia." He picked up her wheeled suitcase by the handle as if it weighed nothing, then turned and disappeared around the corner of the villa.

"I will take you into the villa now," Carmen said. "Please do consider it your home away from home."

"Yes, I'd like that. For now, might I be able to sit, stare at the beautiful view and sip on this amazing drink?"

Carmen smiled. "Of course. I will move your lunch tray to the living room which offers a panoramic view. Please follow me."

Olivia did as Carmen had requested. Who wouldn't be lulled into following. And off they went in the direction of the expansive villa.

Once inside, Carmen offered to give her a tour around and Olivia politely refused. "No thank you, I really would like to just sit and rest." She stretched the truth a bit, and went on to say "I am still a little dizzy from the helicopter ride."

Carmen nodded and showed Olivia into the living room. She did not protest her decision for no tour nor did she offer one for later. Olivia sat down in the rocking chair, planning to go explore later, and convinced she could find her own way around.

As she slowly glided back and forth in the rocker, Olivia realized she was grateful to not be here on the island alone. She'd been a loner since Jane, but she didn't much like being by herself for more than a few hours. Yet, she was not accustomed to services that catered only to her, and it was an uncomfortable feeling.

******

After tucking in lunch, Olivia was drawn outside to discover paradise, its sights and sounds. She made it as far as the deck. There she went to the very edge to check out the view. She held a glass of ice water meant to keep her cool and hydrated in the late August heat.

The balcony on which she stood was made of concrete, surrounded by glass and metal fixtures. It was a perfect complement with nature. It also overlooked a massive pool on the level below. Over the way toward the front of the villa she spotted a beach that included its own calm inlet of lapping water. It sparkled with a slight bluish green hue accented by the sun. Every view of this place she'd seen so far included sand and sea. And there was a breeze constantly blowing. They must be on higher elevation, on a piece of paradise purposefully selected to accentuate the seascape.

Once Olivia was satisfied she'd seen all she could for now, she turned to look for a vantage point to relax. She strategically chose a chaise lounge chair carefully positioned in the shade. It provided protection from the strong rays of the afternoon sun without having to use an umbrella. Opening an umbrella might pose a challenge for her artistic mind, and she was determined not to seek assistance.

Though, the caretakers did seem to be a nice enough pair. They were very quiet as they went about their daily chores without much hoopla.

She'd been watching Pedro tend to landscaping and minor maintenance around the grounds. And while Carmen had not come to check on her, Olivia suspected she controlled all things needing attention in the household. Thus, she was not far away.

Olivia, sprawled out on the lounger and felt she was almost in heaven. This island setting is beautiful. Javier had already mentioned the beach house held every modern amenity: eight bedrooms, nine and a half bathrooms, large eat in kitchen, living and dining rooms, swimming pool, jacuzzi, sauna, and breathtaking views of the sea from every room. He was right, every amenity was accounted for and provided.

Being here was like being king of your own hill. In her case as the Pilot had left her here without him, Olivia considered herself to be queen of the oasis. Hmmm...that would make a great title for a book. Only one thing, rather person, was missing, the Pilot himself.

Olivia got comfortable and even closed her eyes to take in some deep breaths. Both inside and now out here too, every few minutes she found herself looking to the skies, secretly hoping Javier would return after a short while. So far, that had been a hopeless activity. She sighed. Breathe. Relax.

She'd pondered her current situation, unsure if he was ever coming back. *Now, now Olivia,* said her inner voice. *You are being silly. This is his island. He has a staff. Of course he will be back. You just don't know when. He didn't kidnap you, and even if he had, these luxury accommodations are not a hardship. He will come home. The real question is, what will you do when he returns?*

After what seemed like a long time, Olivia felt the shadow of the sun begin to spread across her skin. Noting her lack of sunscreen, empty glass, and desire for air conditioning, Olivia picked up the glass and returned inside.

Slipping through the sliding glass doors into the cool villa, she paddled across the living room, and into the kitchen where she deposited the glass in the dishwasher. She still did not know where Carmen was and yet she could not be far. There was something cooking in the oven that smelled delicious. Opting for a chance to relax a little more, Olivia went back to the living room—fast becoming her favorite room, and she plopped herself down on the couch. She pulled a blanket from the back of the sofa, wrapped herself in it, and laid back. She turned her attention to stare out the window. She sighed...ah, paradise. Almost immediately, she felt herself drifting off to sleep. Naps are good...

******

Javier landed the helicopter as she stood there and waited. "Ms. Olivia?" Wait, why is a woman's voice in this rendezvous?

Disturbing her dreamscape, she heard her inner voice say, *wake up Olivia*. She opened her eyes. Where am I? She looked around as the fog of sleep lifted. Oh, yes! I am on the island, his island in his house and laying on his sofa.

Hours had gone by. She could tell as the placement of the sun had moved again. Now it had begun to set. Olivia remembered she had curled up on the couch and must have fallen asleep staring out the window.

"Ms. Olivia?"

Olivia looked up. There was Carmen, standing a few feet away. She had on her apron and looked to have come from the direction of the kitchen.

"Ms. Olivia?" She heard Carmen say. "I am sorry to disturb you, m'lady? Time for dinner, if you are ready. It is on the dining room table."

She was still laying there with her feet curled under her and the lightweight blanket pulled over her lap. Time for dinner? The day had already gone by...she hoped he'd come home soon. "Yes, thank you" she responded as she lazily got up and folded the blanket. Once that was done, she set it down and paddled in her sock feet to the dining room.

Carmen met her there. "I am sure you are hungry," she said as she put the plate in front of her on the placemat setting. "You didn't eat much earlier and it is getting late." Nothing escaped Carmen's watchful eyes! "Food would be lovely. Thank you! Are you and Pedro going to join me?" Olivia said hopefully.

"Oh no, we will eat at home. Pedro likes to surprise me with dinner most evenings. It's how we keep the sparkle in our relationship."

"A man who cooks?"

"Yes indeed. We fell in love over food. But that's a tale for another day. Sit and eat before it gets cold. If you need anything, ring up the cottage and we'll be here within moments."

"Do you think Javier will come home tonight? Shouldn't I await his return before having dinner?"

"No, I don't believe Mr. Javier will be coming home tonight. I'm sure though he'll be here as soon as he's able. If he does return tonight he'll know to look for leftovers in the refrigerator, and you'll hear his helicopter rotors before landing. Please I request you sit and eat before it gets cold."

"It looks delicious," Olivia said as she sat.

"Thank you Ms. Olivia."

"Oh Carmen, just call me Olivia. We are likely similarly young in age, and I do not want to feel old."

She smiled. "Yes m'lady. I'll do that. Oh, I forgot, I put extra food on another plate for you, if you want a second helping. If not, slide it into the refrigerator and place the dirty dishes in the dishwasher. I'll wash them up in the morning. All the bedrooms have fresh linens including Mr. Javier's. Have a great night and remember if you need anything, just ring."

"I'll be fine. Thank you for everything."

"Tata for now Ms. Olivia! I mean Olivia." Carmen waved as she picked up her keys off the hallway table and walked out the front door.

Olivia turned her attention to her dinner plate. Carmen had been right. She was hungry. The food was divine—grilled fresh snapper, rice with peas and stir-fried vegetables. A glass of white wine. Only thing missing, the Pilot. She sighed as she looked around at the empty chairs at the table. *Oh Olivia, stop pining away and eat!*

When she finished the main course and took her plate in the kitchen, she saw a note on the counter: dessert is rum cake. Have as much as you like. She saw the beautifully baked brown cake sitting inside a glass cake dish. Olivia was stuffed but refused to pass up the cake.

When she'd devoured two healthy slices, and it no longer held her attention, she'd cleaned her dishes and set them in the dishwasher to dry. She put the leftover plate in the fridge, and drank a glass of water.

It was now time to explore this domicile before it got too dark. Olivia wandered from room to room, doing nothing more than looking at the views each room held with its own angle of the sea.

Even though she was curious about so much, there was no need to be an investigator and open closets or drawers. She had lots of questions: what made him pick this island, this home of all the places? Was he hiding out, and why so many bedrooms? Who had decorated the place?

She didn't know how many women the Pilot had brought here to bed. She saw no signs of a 'feminine' presence. That was a good enough sign. Even if it wasn't, there was no pilot or boat captain to take her back to civilization if she couldn't handle the answer— at least not tonight.

At last, Olivia found the master bedroom and walked in. She turned on a floor lamp in the corner. It bathed the room in a soft, soothing light. The master suite was in a wing of its own as a step up three steps. Javier had texted her shortly after he'd left to say don't go swimming alone and feel free to claim his room as hers or pick another one. He was so bossy. Even still, Olivia missed him, his unique lemon zesty scent, his black curly hair, his piercing look and the feel of his hands on her skin...

Shake out of it woman! You are only going to frustrate yourself dreaming about him. True, she agreed with her inner self.

In the middle of the room, was a huge Cherrywood bed. It was fit for a king or the master of this domain. It sat on a pedestal up two steps. The spread was a deep brown and maroon color. Olivia could imagine him as he lay there with sheets barely covering his hips. Keep looking around Olivia!

She went over to look at the view. Even with the sun now gone down and twilight on the horizon, Olivia could see the beautiful seascape of waves washing against the shore. She pulled the cords of the heavy drapes and watched the view disappear. Nightfall had arrived.

Olivia discovered her luggage on a stand in Javier's walk in closet. She moved along lightly touching the wood paneling of the closet drawers, the feel of being in his inner sanctum. She stopped to touch his hanging clothes, robe, flight suits, jackets. She resisted the urge to put his robe on as a way to feel closer to him.

She was still debating back and forth with herself. Should I sleep in his bed or find a room of my own and claim my independence? It was a never ending debate. She yawned. I'm tired! Doing nothing all day takes lots of energy she surmised. Deep down she knew her exhaustion was being fueled by her indecision.

For tonight, how about some peace?

Good idea. She let the debate go, stripped out of her clothes, wrapped herself in a towel she'd seen neatly folded on a stand, and headed for the shower. In the adjoining bathroom, she found everything needed to refresh herself and prepare for a good night's sleep.

After her shower, donned in a robe she'd found on the back of the door, she climbed into the middle of his king-sized bed. It held no smell of him. She was sure Carmen had mentioned she'd already changed the linens. Maybe he'll come back before I awake. She whispered "be safe Pilot wherever you are. Paradise awaits." Olivia fell asleep as soon as her head hit the pillow.

******

Olivia opened her eyes. She felt like she'd been asleep awhile and was finally rested. She looked over at the clock. It's bright blue numbers said 6:12 am. It's

143

definitely morning. She'd slept soundly. She stretched her legs and arms out across Javier's expansive bed. She was definitely alone. No one else had been in bed with her. Instead of dealing with how much she wished he were here next to her, she threw the covers off and went to the window.

She pulled the curtains back and stopped midstream. In front of her, the sea in all its splendor. The sun aglow in hues of red and yellow against the water's horizon. Where sky meets ocean.

Wow, I could get used to this view. She continued to stand there looking out.

After watching the sun rise above the horizon, she again looked at the clock. It said 6:27. Definitely time to get up and stay up. An idea surfaced in her mind: time to take a walk outside and explore the grounds. The Pilot had said don't swim alone. He'd said nothing about walking alone.

She hurried to put on some lightweight clothes. She slipped into a white sundress, some underwear, and flip flops. She purposefully left her hair untied to flow free—I'll deal with this mass of curls later. Now it's my time to go find paradise...

On the main floor, Olivia noticed the house was still silent. It must be too early for Carmen and Pedro to start work. Good news as she didn't want to disturb anyone at this hour.

Which way? She chose to go through the living room— the one doorway she knew where it led and how to keep it unlocked. Once outside, Olivia walked from the deck, down the steps and onto the pool level's patio.

It seemed relatively quiet out here too. She heard a bird make some form of exotic tweet sound, and she could hear the ocean waves gently crashing against the surf. Still even in the early morning, there was a light breeze blowing from the Northwest. Nothing else, no sounds of humanity. Good!

She stepped onto the grass and remembered she had yet to go to the beach and wiggle her toes in the sand. Stop waiting Olivia! Go to the beach! Without further ado, she walked along the backside of the villa beyond the pool and gardens, in the direction where she thought she'd discover the closet beach.

As she walked along, she found a most magical setting hidden from the view of the deck. There on a sandy path peppered with palm trees, it opened up to a small clearing with two big trees on each side of a path, the beach and sea beyond it. Hanging from one of the trees was a big wooden and rope swing. Just after the swing, the path declined downward.

That's odd she thought. Where did it come from, she wondered. Did Javier have it put in or is it remnant of the previous owners? It's quaint. She remembered back to her walk with Javier in Barbados, where they'd come upon the swing and she wanted to go play. She'd passed it up not wanting to make a fool of herself.

Olivia hadn't been on a swing since she was a little girl. There was one just like this one in Jane's yard. If truth be told, being on that swing was her favorite thing to do in her free time as a child. 'Hold on tight and swing for the heavens,' she could still hear Jane's voice as she yelled from the porch. Those were good memories, even after she'd left the wood to rot on the original seat.

As if under a spell, Olivia approached the swing and tugged on the ropes. It seems sturdy enough. It was just about two feet from the ground, so even if it fell with her in it, she wouldn't hurt anything but her ego.

Even though one cannot see the house from here, she looked around to see if anyone was watching. *Olivia, you are being ridiculous! Pride has never stopped you from getting your way. The swing will either hold you or not. Nothing to lose.*

She moved around to the other side and sat down on the thick, wooden beam facing the ocean. So far, so good she said as she looked up into the tree and held herself still. Her focus shifted to the sights before her. She sighed. What a breathtaking view! I could sit here, not moving an inch as the waves lap against the shore in what is a never ending ebb and flow.

No point in going halfway Olivia, her inner voice perked up. *Swing already!*

"Okay fine" she said out loud. Time to test this manmade contraption. She let her flip flops fall to the sand and used her bare feet to push herself backward. Then she let go to glide into the air, her legs straight out in front of her.

Again! Go higher!

Olivia did just that pushing off and sailing forward. She could feel the wind in her hair, billowing the folds of her dress. She laughed aloud. This is glorious. Carefree Olivia was a happy sight indeed.

At some point, Olivia was tired and slowed her pace. She put her feet back on the semi-solid ground of sand and crabgrass. As she gently rocked the swing, she let her feet play in the sand, pink toes gently drawing circles. Ah a quiet calm. Inner peace had swept through her. Nature in its wonder had a way of making you stop to listen. Nowhere to be, nothing to do.

When she was ready to go back to the villa, Olivia got up from the swing. She was convinced she could handle anything now. She had proof: she already dealt with numerous breakdowns and heartbreak in life. Nothing risked, nothing gained. Being on the swing had yet again proven the old adage. She was here risking everything to see where it might lead.

Time to return to his space and await his return...

Chapter 12

"Love can consign us to hell or to paradise, but it always takes us somewhere." ~ Paulo Coelho

It had been a full day in paradise. All morning she worked on her novel. While Carmen did her afternoon housework, Olivia had gone swimming. Carmen promised to keep an eye on her even though Olivia was an expert swimmer. Anything to keep the Pilot from blaming the caretakers. When she'd had enough fun in the sun, Olivia had retreated inside, done more writing, and ate dinner. Carmen had left for the night and Olivia had retired upstairs to get ready for bed.

She had just emerged from the shower, and wrapped one of the fluffy towels around her. Time to dry off, she thought to herself, as she bent down to rub the moisture off her toes. She saw a shadow cross her vision near the bathroom door, and slowly turned her head. "Oh!" she said as she jumped slightly. There he was, the Pilot, standing behind her in the open doorway. She knew she had closed the bathroom door, and locked the bedroom door. She'd thought there was no point in locking both doors as she was alone in the villa, but she also knew not to take unnecessary chances.

"Sorry, I could not resist, querida. I love seeing you in nothing but a towel."

"Be proud of me for not screaming in surprise as I normally would."

"I am, even though it would only be me to hear you." He looked to be perusing over her almost naked body. "I will reward you with a kiss."

Knowing where a kiss was going to lead, to bed, she responded, "no thank you. I do not need to be rewarded for maintaining control. I am learning. You see everything and pop up without warning."

He stepped over to her in two long strides. "Si, querida, I am always watching you with joy. Seeing you in my bathroom in nothing but a towel is such a turn on."

"How did you get in anyway? I locked the bedroom door."

"Ah, Bella mia. This is my house. I keep a master key."

"Of course you do."

"Now, more importantly," Javier whispered in her ear..."have you missed me?"

As much as she wanted to say no, she could not lie. "Yes."

"Good."

She looked into his eyes—beautiful black ones that held such intensity. She was not giving in. "It is so not good.

I feel like you have me wrapped around your little finger."

Javier said, "I would like to have you wrapped around me wearing nothing at all. I imagine your legs encircling my back as I push myself in and out of you."

Olivia watched Javier's eyes slowly move down her body and she suspected she knew exactly what he was thinking. As a matter of fact, as the silent looks continued she felt her body heating up. Why did he have this effect on her. No one had ever been able to breakdown her resolve like he could. Any strategy she had come up with to resist him had failed. *Get a grip Olivia!*

"I thought maybe you were not going to be back so soon. When did you land? I did not hear your helicopter as Carmen said I would. It must be because I was in the shower."

"Si, querida, I just arrived and could not wait to see you before I did anything else. This bathroom has been designed to be soundproof so I can bathe in peace. I too was not sure when duty was going to end. My replacement actually showed up. I could have stayed in the barracks alone and without you tonight. The thought was unbearable. I sleep great with you in my arms, naked and hot."

"Who says I will sleep with you tonight?"

"It is always your choice. I want you in my bed. I imagine if you slept elsewhere, neither of us would get much sleep, or be satisfied."

"You make it sound so logical Javier."

"Ah, but it is very simple. We are insatiable for each other. Male, female, attraction! Stuff happens."

Olivia balled her hands into fists at her sides. "Well tonight, I am going to sleep in another bed. Alone. I do not like the lack of control I seem to exhibit around you. So let's see if we can resist that simple way of stuff happens. I am more than a body to keep you warm and satisfied."

Damn, he did not mean to have been so glib with her. The best of intentions gone awry. He needed to fix this before their relationship spiraled into a direction beyond fixing. He liked her too much as a woman to let her go. She was everything to him right now. He did not understand it, and tomorrow would take care of itself. Now is what matters.

Coming to stand in front of her, he put his hands on her shoulders. "Olivia, please forgive me for what I said. You are not just a female to me. You are an accomplished woman with common sense and a brilliant mind. I will not deny your beauty either. Your body would stop traffic with those amazing curves, luscious

152

lips, soft skin and flowing hair. Oh and I would be remiss if I left out your divine lovemaking skills that make my heart beat so fast."

He paused, and she wanted to scream. As much as it did not feel like she should forgive him for being insensitive, she did love that he saw her that way.

"All I want to do is please you, give you your every desire. In a short time, you've become so important to my sanity. Talking with you provides an objective opinion and gives me perspective. Before you showed up, I always had to be right, and if they dared to contradict me, I would tune them out."

"Thank you for saying that Javier. My upset has nothing to do with you. It's just me, my past and a need to control myself so I don't end up losing myself."

He smoothed her hair gently away from her face. "Olivia, the past is over. We have now, and I want you to know I treasure you as a woman. You are always free to choose. I will honor and respect anything you choose. I am right here for you."

She bit her lower lip and pondered her next words. "I appreciate you Javier. Your patience with me is astounding. For tonight, I will stay with you in your bed..."

Chapter 13

"Sweet, crazy conversations full of half sentences, daydreams and misunderstandings more thrilling than understanding could ever be." ~ Toni Morrison, Beloved

Two weeks later

Javier searched the beach just over the rise from his beach house as he steered his helicopter. Olivia said she would be spending the morning soaking up the sun rays at the water's edge. Not quite sure why she would pick the beach over the pool, he smiled as he thought of how they had made love in the pool lounger yesterday afternoon. Reigning in those thoughts, he looked at his watch to verify the time. Yes, as the big hand moved just to 11 o'clock, he was sure it was still morning.

"Where is she?" He said speaking out loud as he knew she would not go back on her word. He picked up his binoculars to get a better view. Scanning the sandy dunes, he saw her in the distance. No one else would be around on the private beach. There she lay sprawled across the beach chair in a flimsy white dress with her hair flowing free. One look at her instantly excited him. She looked to be reading some sort of book or magazine from behind dark sunglasses. The material of her dress was so gauzy and lightweight that he could clearly make out her shape beneath it. Knowing her wild streak, he was sure the temptress had little or nothing on under it. At that moment all he wanted to do was land the helicopter right there next to her in the sand and make passionate love to her for the rest of the day. Olivia was a vixen who haunted his thoughts and dreams. He could not get enough of her. This tryst was in no way close to being practical and yet he felt alive in her presence for the first time in years, maybe the first time ever. She gave as good as she took, and he was having all kinds of adventures with her inside and outside of his private beach house. Today would be no different and he could not wait to land this helicopter on the helipad, strip down to the minimal amount of clothes he needed to bury himself inside her luscious curves.

******

Across the sand, Olivia sensed that he was nearby. She could just barely make out the sound of the rotors and an engine; looking up from her magazine she could see a helicopter looming on the horizon. It may not actually be Javier, and she would bet the rights to her next novel that it was him. He left the villa in the early hours of the morning long before the sun came up. He had to report for duty at 4 am. After making love last night, she had been exhausted. She had a faint memory of kissing him goodbye, turning over and falling back into a deep sleep. She was unsure how Javier made passionate love to her, slept for a few hours and left for work. She spent most of her days moving from one room to the next, or at the beach or pool. And she could always take an afternoon nap. He on the other hand was driven to work, and rarely took time to rest.

Today was a new day. She kept saying that. And she had been determined to get a couple hours of work done on her next novel before Javier came home. Her agent was expecting the first three chapters in a matter of weeks. Other than the preliminary idea she had sketched out, she had made no progress. The first step to her proven recipe was to research the location of the next romance. It had to take place in an exotic locale. Hence the high-end destinations magazine she was now trying to read. It was not much use trying to concentrate. Every couple of pages she would set it down and close her eyes. Javier was amazing to stare at, trail her fingers over the hard planes of his body, to listen to him talk about his day between kisses and orgasms. She had done things with him, been a different woman, than she had ever done in her life. Just thinking about how much he turned her on warmed her cheeks with a blush. "Scandalous Olivia!" She chastised herself for yet again losing focus on the task at hand.

It had been two weeks of playing in sand with Javier on this amazing private island. Every moment she was away from him, she was reliving the moments they had spent together. The more she resisted, the more she felt she was being pulled into his world—a place where she no longer recognized herself. The Olivia who met the Pilot two weeks ago was self-made, determined, and driven to be independent of any influence a man might have over her mind, body or soul. She wrote about love all day long, and she had no intention of falling in love. One thing was for sure, it seemed as if his presence commanded a response from her body that she had no control over. And here he was coming home for another round. What is it in that old saying? Resistance is futile. She wanted him as she always did and no amount of scolding herself or lack progress mattered.

******

"Well, there you are!"

Olivia looked up from her magazine, pushed her glasses up into her hair, and gave Javier her most devastating smile. "Yes, here I am as if you did not know. I love this beach and I am about a thousand feet away from the spot you found me yesterday!"

He looked down at her and smiled. "Si, so you are!" He paused to look at her from her feet all the way up to her lips, and then up to her eyes, he continued, "I like what I see and don't see." With a gesture to her white cover up, he said, "it looks as if you have on nothing under there. If I am not careful, you are going to be the death of me."

"Stop joking with me Javier, how could I impact your life?"

"You have no idea how distracting you are. I am a trained pro. Otherwise, I would have wrecked my helicopter today when I saw you sitting here in this flimsy gauze cover up. All I wanted to do was this." He

157

took her magazine from her lap, closed it and tossed it over to the other chair.

Olivia watched him squat down and with his right hand push the fabric of her dress up her thigh. At the same time, he leaned his head down and licked her left nipple through the gauzy white material. He found the apex of her heat.

"Si, est bueno. There are no clothes to stop me from doing what I wanted from the moment I saw you here." He pushed his index and middle finger inside her and she lifted herself off the chair to meet the thrust of his fingers.

Olivia moaned. With very little conscious thought she whispered, "what are you doing?"

He stopped sucking on her breast, lifted his head slightly, opened his eyes and looked at her with red hot passion. "I am seducing you querida. Is there any doubt?" He paused and tilted his head slightly as if thinking about what he was doing. "Do you want me to stop?"

With a confused look, she said, "What? Oh no, please don't stop."

He put his free hand where his mouth had been, massaging her breasts all the while continuing to push his fingers in and out with skill and increasing intensity.

Her heart was beating faster and faster. All Olivia could feel was the heat, not of the sun, but of the need burning inside of her for release. A moment later she went over the edge and had one of the most powerful orgasms she had ever experienced. She opened her eyes as the spasms slowed. He was watching her.

"I love to watch you orgasm querida. It turns me on so much. All I want is to strip you and be inside you. I want you, now."

******

Hours later, Olivia awakened to the sun setting over the western horizon. Her head was on Javier's chest, her right leg sprawled over his, and she lay cocooned in his embrace. She would never get enough of being in this Caribbean oasis with its breathtaking views of sunrise and sunset. Nor would she tire of laying with the man of her every dream. He was strong, determined and extremely sexy specimen that would rival the fabled Greek gods of ancient times. Siestas with Javier were mind blowing. The sex was amazing and he did provide for her every need and want in and out of bed. They had barely made it here to his bed before he had dropped his linen pants and buried himself inside of her that first time. They went over the edge together within minutes of coming together. The need to have him possess her was so fierce, and his determination to make love again so complete. The second and third times had been slow and steady. Yet, each time was no less arousing and satisfying.

Olivia knew that she had fallen in love and nothing good could come out of it. For this moment none of that mattered. She was on borrowed time, and never one to cry over spilled milk. He belonged to her, she belonged to him, and all was right in the world. Without being able to stop herself, she reached out to run her hand across his black-haired chest.

Javier could feel her touching him in a far off dream. His arm instinctively tightened around her waist. In a gravelly voice he asked, "Si, what is it querida? You want more?"

"I could not help touching you. More? While it is very tempting to stay here with you, if we do not get up, I think I will starve. Do you have to leave to return to work?"

"No. The storms have ended, and I do not have to leave for a few days to return to my regular duty."

"I am glad the storms ended." Before she could stop herself, Olivia, blurted out. "When you are gone, I worry that you are safe."

"Thank you for being concerned, but do not worry. I am safe now, and the future will always take care of itself."

"You're right!"

"Let's go downstairs. You can keep me company while I make dinner. I gave Carmen the afternoon off. And then after I finish cooking, I will show you how dangerous I can be."

******

Javier had gone outside to take a swim. He was so enamored with her. These few weeks had been unbelievable. He and Olivia has settled into a routine. He went to work and she stayed here and worked on her novel. He was home for a couple of days, and had begun to like not having to leave her. They could take siesta together and act like a normal couple. He had even sat down and relaxed on the sofa, laughing with her as they watched old movies. He couldn't remember the last time he'd indulged in such luxuries, if ever.

******

On another floor in the house there was Olivia perched on the corner of the bed, squeezing or rather punching a pillow, being hopeful she could resolve the internal conflict raging inside her. Javier, so charming, sexy, and giving. Or at least that's what she was feeling. Said another way, hot and bothered. He brought her here, they get along. This is too good to be true.

For at least the hundredth time she asked herself, what is our happy ending? Too many times I've gone to rewrite this book, craving safety, pondering ideas to create a forever breakup. Each time even that idea breaks my heart. Then I remember that I, Olivia, am a romance novelist. It does not work.

Damn you Javier, you get in my head, you call, you walk by. I follow your every move, hang onto your every word. Why am I not immune to you? Why do I keep choosing a no win battle? Who am I kidding? I am not even playing full out for you and yet I act like a love sick puppy when you aren't around. Contained from the outset by my own doing. She said aloud, "I don't like this one bit. I did this with the last one." She paused. "Wait! Maybe you're different. Or maybe I just need to run to the other end of the planet."

Olivia, said that damn voice in her head, *you better get a grip. You are on an island. His island, in his house, sitting on his bed you idiot. I suggest you suck it up and have some fun already!* Ignoring the voice, Olivia punched the pillow again. I can't do this! The voice was still there... *Let go, give in. Come on Olivia. How will we play this? What do you say is possible? That's a laugh....comes back every time to what do we want.* What will you do to have it be? Finally, a rational thought.

She heard that voice in her head again speak, *oh Olivia, you are full of so many questions, just sleep with him again already. It's just sex, and he obviously wants you, can't keep his hands off you. What are you worried about?* Now the voice was asking questions. Frustrated and exhausted, she sighed heavily, fell back on the bed, covered her head with the pillow and whispered, "Lawd, help me! This is setting me crazy!"

A few minutes later, Javier walked into the bedroom talking on his cell phone. She sat up upon hearing his voice. He was standing by the window looking out. She watched him speak in rapid fire Spanish. She did not understand what he was saying as he talking so fast. She thought to herself this is why I wanted to learn Spanish. Taking the Introductory Spanish course three times did not make the difference in actually speaking Spanish, nor did it help being fluent in French. Oh, well it was something to add to her six-page bucket list.

"Why do you want to learn Spanish?"

Coming out of her head, Olivia looked up to see Javier had finished his phone call and was staring at her from across the room. His expression was intense. She had obviously missed something. "Huh?"

"You just said, this is why I wanted to learn Spanish."

She paused to chew on her lower lip. He loved when she did that. It meant she was weighing what she was going to say. What she said next always surprised him as she deliberated being vulnerable versus saying too much.

"Oh! Well I have been trying to learn Spanish for years. I loved visiting Spain and other Spanish-speaking countries. I want to speak and understand Spanish so I know what is happening around me and can communicate. I am no good at Spanish. The way you speak, it is with such passion. I want to learn that way of speaking so the world hears my passion. Anyway, how was your call? It looked serious."

"It was. I have to return home."

"What do you mean, return home? This is your home."

"No, I mean, I have to go back to Spain, to our family home in Jaen."

"Oh, I see." Olivia could not hide the disappointment in her voice. As much as she tried to resist the temptation, she had fallen in love with him, and now he was going back to Spain.

"Olivia, come here please so I may explain."

"You do not owe me any explanations Javier. I am just shocked, that's all. I will go pack."

"No, viene aquí ahora, querida."

"Oh," she clearly understood him repeat the demand in Spanish. As much as she wanted to turn and walk away, there was something in the way he looked at her that propelled her feet across the room to him. She hated herself for being so easy. The men in her books commanded their woman around and that was fine in a silly romance novel. It did not fit her style, or how she lives her life. And here she was standing in front of him as he had summoned her. Viola!

"What is there to discuss Javier? We both knew this thing we have is temporary. You are going home to Spain. I am not staying here to wait for you to come back, even if you did ask, and you didn't. It's time for me to go pack."

She infuriated him with her preconceived notions about what he meant. And yet, she was damn sexy when she was upset. He just wanted to make it better. He just wanted to kiss her midsentence.

"I am not the kind of woman who waits for a man. This was nice and all and…"

Oh hell, who needs to talk. He pulled her into his arms, and kissed her lips midsentence.

Olivia did not want to kiss him back. She could feel his pent up anger ready to boil over. And yet the way his hands pressed her to him, she knew he wanted her as much as she wanted him. She gave in and kissed him

165

back as if there was no tomorrow. There was no tomorrow for them. When he lifted his head, they were both breathless. He leaned his forehead to hers, and she opened her eyes to stare at his feet.

"Olivia, let me explain." He took her hand and pulled her over to the couch. He sat down placing her onto his lap.

She opened her mouth to speak, and he put his finger up to her lips.

"Olivia, please hear me out." She nodded her head as she agreed to listen. "I just talked to my father. My mama is sick, and has to have surgery in four days. I am going home to be with her, and help out in any way possible. We are a very close family, even though we live all over the world. My place is to be there."

She looked into his sad eyes and it melted her heart. "I understand Javier and I am sorry to have acted like a child."

"No, Olivia, you do not understand. It was while talking to my father about how scared he is that my mother will not recover, that I realized how much he loves her and cannot stand the idea of living without her. I tried to alleviate Papa's fears, tell him she would be okay, and that he was not talking rationally. Papa said to me, 'when you love someone as much as I love your mama, then you do not want to imagine a day when you will

166

not see them, be with them, or even how to take the next breath without them.' He told me that someday perhaps I would know that kind of love."

"I hear how much he loves your mother."

"Yes, he does. In dealing with my mama being sick when she has always been so healthy, in having to go home, and with my papa falling apart, all I could think about is I do not want to leave you."

Olivia put her hand on his cheek. "Yes, I get you do not want to leave me. You owe me nothing. Just be however you are, deal with this crisis and I will be fine. You are going home to be with your family. It is right."

Javier ran his left hand through his hair. "Look, I want you to come with me."

"No, Javier. It is not appropriate."

"Look at me Olivia Stevenson. I love you."

She looked into the depths of his eyes. Eyes she could drown in. She was hearing words that she wanted to hear. "No, Javier you are emotional and worried about your parents."

"I want you to come with me because you have my heart. I get all of this is sudden, and it might seem like I am just saying this because of what my dad said. Maybe it is why I am saying it now. I have been selfish and secretly loving you. I have been in love with you since the first day we met and I did not tell you. I am a proud man and do not know how to say what I feel. At least, not until now."

"What? It is not possible you love me! You do not know me. It is just the sex."

He laughed out loud. Shifting her off his lap, he sat her on the table in front of him. She was exciting him. "Really, Olivia? I get I have indeed shocked you. Do you think I would invite just any woman to my private island? I own a helicopter and have the resources to have stayed in Barbados indefinitely or leave without saying goodbye. I can be anywhere I want in the world. I wanted to be with you. I want to be with you. Come home with me, please?"

She wanted to believe him. "If I go with you back home, what will your family think?"

"They will think I am a blessed man to have you by my side to see me through. They will see the love I have for you when I look at you, and hold you close. They will think I am lost, and they will tell me to do whatever I have to in order to keep you in my life."

Biting her lip, Olivia looked away and pondered if he was serious or not. What his family thought mattered to him, that much she was sure of. She did not have much experience in expressing her love. Was this the moment to tell him she loved him too? No, she needed to be sure this was not some passing feeling. If he did not really love her, it would break her heart. "This is all so sudden. I do not know what to do."

"Look, you get to choose. You do not have to love me and I get we may not be together beyond here on this island. Just know there is enough of me to love you even if you do not return my love. When we are together, what we create is amazing. You have my word I will not pressure you to come to Spain, stay here, or go. You are free to choose what you want. I cannot promise though that I will not come find you when this crisis with my family is over. I get what I want, and I want you."

"Javier, I will go with you to Spain."

Chapter 14

"I'm always sad to leave paradise, but I leave behind the hopes of coming again soon." ~ Irina Shayk

Javier and Olivia set out and left his island via helicopter about six o'clock the next morning. She selected her pink sweatshirt, yoga pants, underwear, socks and sneakers for the long journey. His brother, Juan Carlos, had sent the company jet to fly them back to Spain. It had arrived in the early hours of the morning back in Barbados. Shortly after clearing the customs area reserved for those travelling for corporations or the ridiculously rich, they boarded the gulf stream G550 plane. Climbing the stairs seemed like a chore. Neither of them had slept much the night before. Javier did not come to bed until well after midnight. Olivia had packed, tried to relax into sleep before he came to bed and was not successful. All she could think about was Javier saying he loved her. She was so unsure of what to do next. It was so unexpected. She should be happy, excited. She was petrified.

When Javier finally climbed into bed, they spent a little while talking about the procedure his mother needed for her heart. It was risky, and no one knew if it would be successful. His mother could die, and he was not ready to deal with that reality. For the most part though they just lay in bed holding one another and listening to the other breathe. As soon as Olivia fell asleep it seemed it was time to get up. She had never been a fan of getting up before sunrise.

Somberly they had dressed in silence and it seemed as if they were both a million miles away. The ride back to the mainland was quick and all Olivia remembered was the noise being made by the rotors on the chopper. Now aboard the elegant jet, she was seated, strapped in and ready for the seven hour flight. They were due in about 3 o'clock in the afternoon. From the airport, they would go right to the private clinic to see his mother. He had explained that she would remain there for another night, and she had somehow convinced the doctors to let her return home for two days until her procedure at a hospital in Barcelona.

Javier came to stand in front of her. "Querida, we are about to take off. Are you ready to return home with me?"

"Yes," she lied. She was so not ready to face whatever there was to deal with halfway around the world.

He leaned over and hugged her, placing a kiss just above her right shoulder. He then kissed her on the lips in a quick peck. "I could kiss your lips, kiss you all over. Now is not the time. We have been cleared to go. I promise soon enough I will show you my home country and make love to you in places that will have you never forget how much I love you." He let her go, straightened up, and strapped himself into the seat across from her. The plane taxied and they took off for destination: Granada, Spain about sixty miles from Jaen.

171

At the airport, they were picked up in a black limousine and taken to a private clinic. Javier held her hand each step of the way. When they walked into a separate wing of the private clinic, aptly named as the Santos and Catalina Gutierrez Clinic, Olivia started to wonder more about his family. Obviously they were very important to this part of Spain. She would just bet there was some family relation to the name of the clinic. She started to chew on her bottom lip, and realized she was not easily breathing. Javier must have noticed too as he leaned over and whispered to her, "relax querida, I am right here. My familia will love you just as I love you."

She took a deep breath. "Thank you for saying that." After turning the corner at the end of a long hallway, Javier paused in front of the nurses' desk. He spoke in rapid fire Spanish and Olivia suspected he was asking where he could find his mother's room. The nurse responded and pointed off to the right. She heard him say 'gracias.' He then turned to Olivia and spoke, "the nurse said Mama is resting in her room. Let's go see her." He pulled her close, placed his hand on the small of her back, and moved them toward the direction the nurse had pointed.

In front of a room that must have been the right one, Javier stopped and pushed open the door. Inside was a woman laying on the hospital bed with monitors hooked up to her and medicine dripping into an IV. Every few seconds the machine emanated a soft beep.

Javier's mother was an elegant woman with her hair tied up in a simple bun atop her head. While she had a few streaks of grey that mixed into her jet black hair, she did not look to be old enough to have adult children. Her eyes were closed when they walked in. By her side, with his head resting next to her and his hand covering hers, was an older version of Javier. Olivia suspected it was his father. It was a very personal scene into which they seemed to intrude. She whispered quietly to Javier, "they are sleeping, we should not wake them."

He whispered back into her ear, "I am here now, I want them to know I have arrived."

His mother must have sensed her son was nearby, as she opened her eyes. In English, she said "my son, you are here."

"Si Mama, I had to come."

"I told your father and brothers not to worry you."

She rubbed her free hand into the hair of Javier's father. She smiled. "And I am happy you are here."

At the movement, his father must have awakened. He lifted his head as if fighting sleep.

"Yes, Mama, of course I am here. Hello Papa."

His dad rose from the chair and moved around the bed. He shook his son's hand and said, "Javier, welcome home. It is good to see you, mi hijo. And who is this beautiful woman by your side?"

"Yes, little one, I raised you not to be rude. Please introduce your lady friend."

Javier pulled Olivia to stand in front of him. "Mama, Papa, please meet my Olivia!"

"Olivia, what a beautiful name for a jewel like you! I am Antonio. His father reached out and lifted her hand to his lips. It is a pleasure to meet you. My son has exquisite taste to have picked you as his Olivia. Did you know that Olivia means olive in Española?"

His mother cut him off. She smiled. "Olivia, ignore the charmer that my husband is. He means no harm and is always charming around alluring women. I am Catherine. I am a little sickly right now. The doctors tell me they have it all under control and I will be as good as new in no time."

"It is nice to meet you, ma'am. I hope that you are well soon. And also to meet you Senor Gutierrez."

"Please call me Catherine or Mama or anything other than ma'am. That title makes me feel old. And call Antonio that or Papa."

"Yes ma'am. I mean Catherine. I will."

Antonio had let go of Olivia's hand and hugged Javier. "Welcome back my son."

Totally ignoring the men in the room, Catherine spoke rather loudly to no one in particular. "It's wonderful my son brought you home to meet us before he married."

Javier's father turned to frown at his wife. "Catherine...stop!" He went back over to his chair and sat down. Without turning his focus off Catherine, he said rather pointedly, "Bella, I do understand you are sick, and still that does not excuse you to say anything that is on your mind. Olivia is a guest."

"Olivia, please excuse my outburst. It's just that my son Juan Carlos got married without telling us or even introducing us to the woman he loved. They eloped and came home after the honeymoon. We had a religious blessing in our family's church and big reception. I was disappointed to say the least that they could not wait or come home to Spain to marry."

Olivia did not know what to do or say next. She felt Javier squeeze her hand and then he spoke.

"Mama, let's not rehash any of that right now. We came here to the hospital for a short visit and do not want to tire you out. There will be plenty of time to get to know Olivia after your surgery."

Catherine sighed. "I suppose you are right. Now is not the time. And this nice young woman does not need to listen to my rant. I am so happy that you are both here."

Javier did not loosen his grip on Olivia's hand. "Thank you Mama."

"The two of you go to the palazzo and get some rest. You have had a very long journey from America. I am sure Juan Carlos had your room made up for you both. Go now. I am tired."

"Okay Mama. Papa. We will be back tomorrow."

"Lovely querida, and I may be home before you come back. The doctor actual believes I can come home for a couple of days before the procedure. He thinks it will lighten my stress being in a familiar place."

Javier looked over to his father who quietly nodded his assent.

"Very good. Be well Mama." Javier still holding Olivia's hand, leaned over and kissed Catherine on her forehead. They made their quick goodbyes and slipped out of the room.

In the hallway, Olivia looked up into Javier's face. She could sense the strain seeing his mother was causing. Just below his set jaw, and determined look was a slight glimpse of fear. Wanting to keep the mood light, Olivia said "your parents appear to be in sync with one another, with lots of bantering back and forth."

"Oh yes, when life throws one a curvy futbol, they bring humor."

Olivia laughed at his joke. Then she asked, "how come they were speaking in English?"

"They practice their English all the time. Mama says that Papa promised her a mansion in North America when her English is perfecto!"

"Wow, a mansion!"

"My father often indulges my mother with whatever she wants. Of course she does not like to ask for anything. It frustrates him, so he plays little games to challenge her to share her heart's desires."

"That's fun. What was that whole thing about your brother getting married? You did not lie to your parents and tell them we are engaged?"

Javier laughed. "Oh no, nothing like that. It is a long story. Let's just say that Mama is a control freak and wants things to go her way. I will let Juan Carlos and Lacey fill you in on the rest of it."

"Oh okay." Olivia was not sure what all that was about. Javier seemed to find amusement in her question, so she did not see any reason to worry over it right now.

"Javier, welcome home!" Olivia heard someone say behind her back. She turned around to face the voice. A man that looked like a combination of Catherine and Antonio stood a few feet away. Olivia suspected it to be one of Javier's five brothers.

Chuckling aloud, Javier whispered. "Speak of the devil, himself." With that acknowledgement, Olivia knew that Juan Carlos was before her.

"Thanks Bro." Javier moved from behind Olivia and stepped forward to hug his brother.

Then he slapped Javier on the back. "I see you arrived safely and have been in to see Mama. And this gorgeous woman must be Olivia."

Olivia smiled. "Thank you and buenos tardes."

Reaching out a hand to Olivia, he said "I am the handsome and smart brother. My name is Juan Carlos."

"Don't believe him Olivia. He makes up all kinds of stories to inflate his ego."

She smiled and knew the banter did not end with their parents. She suspected all six brothers were quite a comedy of laughs when in the same vicinity. She had a little bit of humor in her too.

"It is wonderful to meet you. How come I did not get a hug like your brother? After all the hours I spent flying here on your plane, we are family now."

"Javier, I like her already. She will fit in great with the brood."

"Yes she will," Javier said agreeing with his older brother.

"How is Mama?"

"She seemed good, in spite of all the machines that say otherwise. She was definitely in rare form. You and Lacey will owe Olivia an explanation about how you got married." Javier quirked up his lips in a suppressed smile.

"Not that, still. Mama said something didn't she."

"Yep she sure did!"

Juan Carlos looked like he had been chastised. The smile gone from his face. "Olivia, I apologize for my mother's behavior. I am indeed the culprit, and it looks like I will never live down my faults. I promise that Lacey and I will share our story while you are here."

"It is none of my business about your marriage."

"To the contrary Olivia. We do not have any secrets in this family. You are a part of the family now, remember?"

Javier hoped Olivia was starting to understand that she really was now a part of his family. "Speaking of family, where is Lacey? Where are Alberto, Tomas Miguel, Marcelo and Leandro Cruz?"

"Lacey is at the store. She told me I needed to come alone to spend some time with the parents. Always the logical one. She is determined to bake some chocolate dish for dessert that calls for Belgian chocolata." Turning his focus to Olivia, he said, "my wife loves chocolate. You might say she is a connoisseur of all things chocolate."

Not able to contain himself, Javier said, "no truer words were ever spoken."

Continuing on, Juan Carlos said "I am not sure where Alberto is at present. Probably in the olive groves fussing at the workers tending the trees as they prepare for the December harvest. LC was here earlier this morning. Marcelo will arrive tonight from Paris, and our TM is sleeping off a night of partying in Barcelona. Each of us promised to stop by for only a few minutes so as to give Mama and Papa time alone and for her to rest. You know when we are in the room she is bossing us around, asking all kind of questions, doing that motherly thing."

"Oh boy, do we know!"

"You headed back to the palazzo?"

"Yes, we are tired from traveling. You know I had to see Mama before going home."

"Smart move. I will see you both back at the homestead. Your bedroom has been made up for you and I hope you will be comfortable. We all have to keep up our strength for Mama. Olivia, it is great to meet you, and I promise to keep my word about our story." Not waiting for a response, Juan Carlos then moved past them and disappeared into the room.

Chapter 15

"Intimacy is not purely physical. It's the act of connecting with someone so deeply, you feel like you can see into their soul." ~ Reshall Varsos

"Come here sweetheart."

She walked over to where he stood with his arms open for her to step into the warmth she knew they held for her. It had been a whirlwind of activity since they had stepped off the airplane. Olivia loved flying and yet this trip had been different. She had been anxious and worried about Javier's mom, what his family would think of her, and what it would be like to visit under these circumstances. She was unsure of what to expect, especially with his mom's illness. Crazy enough, everyone was accepting of her and even seemed content with her sharing his bedroom. She could not escape the feeling that she did not belong here, or perhaps she just thought to pinch herself for how amazing it was to be here with Javier.

They had just been dropped off at the palazzo, the place where Javier had lived, was raised and shaped into the man he is today. From the outside, it looked like a castle with many, many rooms.

"You did not ask me for a tour!"

"Was I supposed to just demand a tour, especially with all that was going on, checking on your mom, and meeting your family?"

"You're right querida. Let me give you a tour of the palazzo, or perhaps just my suite of rooms." He looked at her with a look that told her exactly what he wanted.

"You have a one track mind, Javier! Yes, please give me a tour of anything you want me to see."

He stopped holding her and she immediately felt a loss of warmth. Just as quickly he reached out and captured her hand in his. "Come…"

Off they went. The pace was slow with occasional pauses to peek inside a room here or there. As he explained the different areas of his family home, Olivia could not help wondering what it would be like to raise children here on the edge of olive groves. She loved the layout, spacious yet welcoming. She could see why this was the central meeting space for their big family. She would get lost if she wandered out alone. As he talked, she tried to commit as much as she could to memory. The way Javier was rubbing his thumb across her wrist, it was hard to concentrate. His whispers in her ear each time they stopped was like a purr of a cat. He was making her blush as he shared what he wanted to do to her body in each room of the house.

"Javier, stop teasing me."

Smiling he said "oh my Olivia, I will make good on each word. There is no need to tease you. You have my promise."

"What would your family think if they heard you talking like this?"

"My family knows how I am when I go after what I want. I am determined, patiently planning, executing my plan and soon enough I will have my way. What's not to love?"

"Cute, Javier! What makes you think I will fall into your honey trap?"

He laughed loudly. "You are so direct. It's all good. I love that you say exactly what's on your mind."

"Well, I cannot help it. I sometimes wonder if it even matters if I am with you. It all goes according to your plan. What happens when you get tired of me?"

"I will never get tired of you."

"So are you saying you like everything there is to like about me?"

"I don't know whether I will like everything about you. Yet, I probably will. You are like a breadth of fresh air."

"Well thank you Javier. I believe you are pretty special too."

"Thank you querida."

They walked for what seemed like forever. Now they were on the second floor. She noticed she was starting to get tired. Looking at her reflection in a mirror as she went by, she could see that she had dark circles under her eyes. She supposed the couple of hours of restless sleep on the plane could do that to someone. Even though exhausted, she was actually enjoying herself. Javier mentioned earlier the remaining family members would show up between tonight and tomorrow. She wondered to herself what they will be like? What unique traits will they have? How would mealtime go with six brothers, a couple of wives/girlfriends—would they all fit at one table?

Javier stopped and she almost bumped into his back. Turning around, he smiled down at her. "Look! Here we are at my suite."

"How convenient!"

"I see you are tired, so I am glad we are at a place where we can rest for a while."

"Rest? Really…"

"Come." He said it again.

Here in his native country, he liked to use that phrase. Who was she trying to fool? It did not matter what he said, she would follow him like a puppy dog begging for attention from its master.

He opened the door and moved aside for her to pass. She stepped into a room decorated in deep mahogany wood and blue hues. In the center of the room was a giant king sized, four poster bed. Off to the right was an ensuite bathroom with walk in shower, Jacuzzi tub, and double vanity sink. There was a sitting area and another door that she presumed led to a closet.

She was impressed. "You're suite is beautiful."

"Correction, for as long as we are here, this is our suite. Whatever you need, it will get fulfilled. You simply have to ask, and it shall be done. Now, what can I get for you?"

"May I have a glass of water?"

"Yes, absolutely. I will go get it. Until I return, make yourself at home." He turned and walked out the door, gently closing it behind him.

She went over and sat down in the brown winged back leather chair, part of a set that included an ottoman. It looked to be the perfect area in which could curl up with a good book. Just beyond the furniture were French doors that led out onto what looked to be a balcony. In the distance Olivia could see the sun setting over the olive groves. She had seen some amazing sunsets as she traveled the world. And yet this one was quaint and peaceful—unto itself breathtaking.

"Why are you there?" He asked as he came back into the room carrying a glass of ice water and approached her.

She looked away from the windows to where he stood just in front of her. "What do you mean?"

He handed her the glass, and she took a tentative sip of water. She could see he was closely watching her. "Why are you sitting in the chair?"

"It seemed like a great place to wait."

"Why did you not get on the bed? We both know you are tired. Are you afraid to be in my bed?"

"No, I just didn't want to mess it up." She took a gulp of water not sure if she really was afraid to be in his bed, this bed in his family home.

Shaking his head, he walked over, took off his shoes, and climbed on the bed with the grace of a lion going to rest in its lair.

"Come over here, Olivia."

"Okay." She set her glass down on the coffee table and walked over to the bed as if in a trance. She took off her sneakers, climbed high atop on the four poster bed and sat down. She purposefully left a foot of distance between them.

"Wow, this bed is high off the ground."

"Yes, it is. It has been my bed since I was nine years old. It is an heirloom in my family. Each of us brothers has a similar bed in our rooms. When we were little boys, too grown for our own good, Mama had an antique dealer find six matching beds. Most of us at the time, we were not tall enough to climb up without help. We even had stepping stools. She used to say that we would have 'big shoes to fill to be the kind of man our father is so why not start early.' None of us knew exactly what she meant at the time. And then these beds arrived. We had lots of fun climbing up and jumping off. We got into lots of trouble as well."

"I bet you all were a handful!"

"Little by little Mama taught us life's lessons. Now that we are all grown, and some of us with our own families, we are starting to see what it takes to run the family business, pursue our own dreams, care for those we love, spend time together as a family and give back to those less fortunate than ourselves."

"I like your mom. She is wise beyond her years. When she saw you today, she had the biggest smile on her lips. Even though sick, she was not able to hide how much she loves you."

"Yes, she is wise for sure. I love my mother. At times, she is downright demanding and bossy. I guess that is how she loves us. Always questioning what we are up to, how we are giving back to society, when will we settle down, what legacy we plan to leave behind, and on and on. My father often reminds us she will get what she wants one way or another."

Olivia smiled across at him. "She gets the temporality of life. Born to live for the time you live and then to die. I think she taught you well how to get your way too."

"Yes, coming from a big family, we definitely have a 'joi de vie' that she instilled in us all. I never resisted the lessons she wanted to teach us. Two of my brothers, Alberto and Juan Carlos, they resist everything. Alberto is a firestorm of passion and drama; Juan Carlos hides out. Alberto has always stayed here to run the family business. He gets an extra dose of her love, more than the rest of us. He will even joke with us that we left him behind to suffer."

"And what does your mom say to that?"

"She says he is a gluten for punishment. She has been teaching him for too many years to mind her, and still he will not go without a fight."

"From what little I saw of your mother's opinion of Juan Carlos' marriage, she stays connected."

"Si, never a dull moment around here querida."

"What about your other three brothers?"

"Tomas Miguel and Marcelo. They are, how do I say, calmer. Marcelo does whatever Mama asks. He is always making the rest of us look bad when he is around. Even now, married, whenever our parents call he shows up to save the day. He stayed close by until recently. He now lives in Paris, with his wife Elaina and her children from a previous marriage. They are expecting their first child in 7 months.

"Tomas Miguel is a playboy. We do not ever expect him to settle down. He travels the world being seen with beautiful women and partying. He was last said to be in Monte Carlo before coming back home yesterday. In addition to all the homes the family owns and are at his disposal, he has apartments in Roma, New York, and Sydney. He only comes home when there is an emergency or Mama begs him to come see her. He says she will always be his first and only love."

"That's precious." She said thinking what is would be like to have so many children.

Leandro Cruz, or LC for short, he is business minded. Nothing ever comes before business. He lives mostly in Barcelona. He is a very private man, and does not share much information about his personal   side. Mama often cuts him the most slack. It's like she's afraid he'll just bury himself more in his work. Juan Carlos was sort of like that until he met Lacey."

He reached over and rubbed the sleep out of her left eye; his thumb gently caressing the skin just below her eyelid. She could not help but close her eyes and let herself feel him touching her.

"Enough stories about my family," he said. "It's time for you to rest."

"Hmmm, I'm okay."

"No! It's time to rest."

"I am not a baby, Javier."

"I know querida. Let me take care of you, spoil you, love you. You are a guest in my family's home. It is customary that you be treated as such. Go take a hot, relaxing shower. You will find soft, fluffy towels next to the shower, any toiletries you want are under the sink, and there is a robe on the back of the door."

"Why don't you come with me?"

"Oh, Olivia, if I go with you into the shower, we will not be relaxing. We will be hot, steamy and passionate all over the bathroom and for many hours. While I would like nothing more than to devour you, tomorrow will be a long day. All in due time, I promise."

"What are you going to do while I am in the shower?"

"I am going to call to say goodnight to my parents and check on Mama's condition. Then I too will be taking a shower."

Olivia wanted to go to bed, and she also wanted to stay up. "But, it's only 8:00 pm, too early to bed down for the night. What about food? You should be the one to use your shower?"

"You are rambling. What you say about bedtime is perhaps true for us if we had not traveled for eleven hours. Mama on the other hand, is under strict orders to rest early and often. Now go! I will take care of everything. The cook will have set aside food for us, and I will shower in the other bathroom."

"What other bathroom?"

Javier jumped off the bed and walked to the door on the opposite end of the room. The one she thought was a closet. He opened the door to another smaller bathroom that had an adjoining door. "Voila!"

"Two bathrooms?"

"When we were little, there were many of us, so Mama had help. Papa was too busy in the fields to see to all our needs. We had a nanny for many years."

"Interesting! Very well, you win. A shower would be nice. Tell your parents thanks again for letting me stay and I will look forward to seeing them tomorrow."

"That's my feisty Olivia, giving in to common sense." She was about to protest when he covered the distance separating them and took her lips and drew her into a passionate kiss. All her resolve melted away with the kiss. When they came up for air, she whispered "see you soon."

"Si, have a great shower; think of me."

She floated out of the room on cloud nine to the bathroom. Once inside she contemplated locking the door. She decided against it. Still getting used to a man willing to put her needs before his own. She did admit she loved the idea of wrapping herself up in his robe. For a brief second she had a flicker of doubt that such a man actually existed and was paying attention to her as if she really mattered. She chastised herself saying aloud "Olivia, you've got to stop mistrusting every man who wants to get close to you. Good point!"

After a wonderfully long shower, Olivia emerged from the bathroom to find Javier under the covers asleep in the bed. His wet curls looking tame as the angelically framed his face. He is so handsome.

Looking around, she saw a tray of snacks and fruits. She was not hungry. Not sure what to do in the dimly lit room, she relished the idea of sliding under the sheets with him. She was already warm from the shower. The idea of being in the bed naked with him was heating her body temperature from warm to hot at lightning speed.

By the time she made her way across the room and over to the bed, she was on fire. "Javier, you sleep?"

"Hmmm?"

"You sleep?"

"Almost. I was waiting for you. I too am tired so I closed my eyes for a moment."

She reached out to run her index finger across his cheek. "Well you almost never sleep. All the worry about your mother has kept you up even more. We both need sleep."

"Si, you are right." He reached out and held open the covers to invite her in.

She hesitated unsure whether to snuggle in with the robe or take it off. "Should I leave the robe on or not?"

"I don't have any clothes on, so why should you."

"Will you keep me warm?"

"Si. Lose the robe, and get in."

Olivia opened the robe to Javier's tired, yet appreciative eyes. She put it at the bottom of the bed, and climbed under the covers and into his arms.

"I have waited all day to have you naked in my arms. My woman, right here with me, where you belong." She wiggled her body into his and could feel his erection pressing against her stomach.

"Javier, I thought we said we were tired and going to sleep."

"We did, and our bodies seem to have a different idea."

"I am tired." She found herself rubbing her forehead as if undecided. And then she leaned over and whispered into his hear. "And what I really want is you to make love to me."

He pulled her up on top of him. "Your wish is my command." He kissed her with a reckless passion that awakened her. She felt herself getting more and more aroused. She moved her hand down his body to hold his erection in her hand. Stroking back and forth she could hear his moaning or was that her?

"How bout we skip foreplay for now. I just want you inside me."

"You are reading my mind." With that declaration, his erection found her core, and he pushed inside. With all the remaining energy she had, she met each thrust he gave such that the intensity of the orgasm building up inside her came so fast. She heard him whisper, "I do not want to come yet."

"Me either. It feels so good. You feel so good inside me."

Neither of them stopped the reckless abandon that had them wanting completion so they would be fully spent. Moments later, Olivia could hold back no more. As she called out his name, he too let go and came inside her with the last of his strength. Their breathing heavy, all she wanted to do was lay there and not move. He stroked her back up and down as their breathing slowed. The last thing she heard before falling into a deep sleep was Javier saying "goodnight querida." They slept.

The next morning, he awoke with Olivia in his bed. It wasn't a dream. How fortunate he was to have her here with him. Soon enough his mother would have a major surgery and his Olivia would be by his side to see him through. That was a greater comfort than he thought it could ever be. Loving her was giving him a new purpose in life.

She must have sensed he was awake as she began to wake up. "Good morning querida."

"Good morning you!" She turned so she was staring up at him.

He looked down into her blue eyes. They mesmerized him with their shimmer that reminded him of the blue ocean, vast and deep. An idea formed. He smiled. "Come go to the beach with me Olivia? I want to show you the Mediterranean coast. And maybe in our adventures, we can find a private spot, for just the two of us. You know, like being back on my island.

Olivia was tempted to give in, especially when he reminded her of their reckless abandon on his island. However, it was pointless to pretend that his mother's health issues weren't serious. "No, Javier! We cannot up and disappear to frolic at the beach! We just got here yesterday. Our job is to look after your mother and visit with your family. I already am enough of a distraction to them without you trying to seduce me."

He kissed her slowly and with no doubt to what was on his mind.

Pulling away to a sitting position, Olivia pleaded, "Javier stop! When you kiss me like that I cannot think."

"What's wrong with that," he lifted his brow as if he were innocent.

"One of us has to be the voice of reason. We need to go to the hospital to help your father bring your mother home for a few days so they get some rest."

"Fine, you are right querida. I will let you win, for now! But mark my words, we will go to the beach after Mama comes home. I will make love to you many times just as I did in Barbados, and on my beach." He pulled her back into his arms and whispered in her ear, "I want you, and I will have you."

Olivia went to respond and thought better of it. She knew she wanted him and had no desire to resist. Damn, he is so sexy when he's being bossy. She shook her head in agreement and looked forward to his mother's improving health.

******

Javier's parents did indeed come home later that day. Javier had gone off to get them settled in, leaving her alone with the promise of only being gone about an hour. Olivia had told him she was going to the library and write. She had been there only for about twenty minutes when she heard the door open.

"Hi Olivia. Got a minute?"

She looked up to see Juan Carlos coming into the library carrying a couple of glasses filled with an opaque liquid.

"Sure. What do you have there?"

"I brought you some homemade lemonade" he said as he handed her the glass.

"You made it?" She said as she took a sip.

"Gosh, no. I do not have culinary skills at all. As a matter of fact, Lacey has banned me for trying to cook anything."

"That is unfortunate. Thank you for bringing me lemonade. It is very good. What's up?"

"Did you know tomorrow is Javier's birthday?"

"Ummmm no, I did not."

"I didn't think so."

"Why do you ask?"

"Well Mama wants to have a family dinner, and Javier said no. I was hoping you might convince him to say yes. You know, work your feminine whiles."

Olivia began to turn red, not quite sure what forms of persuasion Juan Carlos might think she had over his brother. "Oh? I do not think I have the power to convince Javier to do what he has already said no to."

"I disagree. I see how he looks at you Olivia. I do not like to endure my own birthday celebrations. I am not asking because I want my brother to have a celebration he is opposed to. Our parents sacrificed so much for us. It's our turn to pay it back. I am asking because I think it will cheer up Mama and put her in a good mood before her surgery at the end of this week. Mama deserves some happy moments and a few hours is worth it to accomplish that for her."

"I am sure she would love to have her entire family at a dinner. The doctor says it's okay?"

"Yes, the doctor said as long as she did not do any work, it was a good idea. She was disappointed when Javier said no, and she asked me to convince him. I am probably not the best one to do that as I would just tie him up and hold him hostage."

"Yes, that would probably upset both Javier and your mother."

"I'm sure."

"I can't make any promises Juan Carlos, but I'll do my best to make him see the light."

"Thank you! Let me know if you need any assistance. Worst case we will have the family dinner without him. Mama will not be pleased and we'll distract her with as much love as we can."

"Okay. I appreciate your asking and for the lemonade."

"Olivia, it is I who owes you. Now I must go. Lacey is probably wondering if I snuck back to work. I will leave you to keep working." And with that he found his way out.

Olivia continued to sip on her lemonade after Juan Carlos left pondering on the situation. She had no idea how to bring up the subject with Javier. True he had not mentioned to her tomorrow was his birthday, and she did not mind. For Olivia, everyday should be treated as if it is a birthday, a celebration to be alive. Yet most people only celebrated once a year and Javier's mother wanted a celebration. They came all this way to support her, and having the birthday dinner was just another facet of keeping her happy.

Olivia sighed. It really was none of her business and she had given her word to Juan Carlos. So she would see it through. The direct approach was probably the best. When Javier returns, she would address it.

She stood and went over to stare out at the olive groves in the distance from the palazzo. She had a new challenge. What would she give Javier for a birthday gift? On such short notice in finding out tomorrow was his birthday, she did not have time to go shopping for a gift. Even after knowing him for a little over a month, she had no idea what he needed or wanted. Then as if a little birdie whispered into her ear, she had an idea. She is a romance novel writer after all. She would write Javier a love note with three simple words on it, I love you.

Pleased with herself for coming up with the perfect gift, she went to the desk, opened the top drawer, found stationery and an envelope. She sat down at the desk, and picked up a nearby pen. She hoped no one would miss these items and she doubted they would. It was only plain paper with no distinguishing marks. Javier would for the first time know her true feelings for him. She was tired of hiding her love for him. She had immediately bonded with his brothers and parents. They had welcomed her with open arms as if she belonged at his side. Javier had been right about them and she felt loved. She put the note inside her notebook determined to keep it safe while she figured out how to present it at the right time.

A short time later, Javier, true to his promise came to the library. "I'm back!"

"How are your parents doing?" she asked from where she sat on the sofa.

"They are good. Mama is very happy to be in her own home, even if it is short lived before her procedure. The medical team set up what was needed to get her through and the doctor promised to stop in tomorrow for a 'house call.' They will have a quiet evening."

"Why didn't you mention tomorrow is your birthday?"

Frowning down at her, he said, "How do you know tomorrow is my birthday?"

She could see the controlled anger in his question. "Juan Carlos mentioned it. He said you did not want to celebrate it with your mom being sick. He hoped I might convince you to change your mind. And your mom wants to have a family dinner."

"Well I don't." He ran his hand through his hair. "It is just another day. He had no right to tell you and my mom is already in frail health that she doesn't need anything else to focus on other than getting well."

"Maybe it will make your mom feel better to have something happy to celebrate."

"Look, stay out of this. I will have my words with Juan Carlos for dragging you into our family business."

"Oh, so once you make up your mind, it's butt out, huh?'

Coming to stand in front of Olivia, Javier pulled her up into his arms, tilted her chin up so he looked into her eyes. "Querida, I am sorry for behaving like a child." She saw the sparkle in his eyes as he added. "We are even now, si?" Then his expression turned serious. "I love you as if you are a part of me, so no my mind is not made up. I will listen to your opinion. I suspect my brother knew this and he put you in the middle of it."

"Well I do not know what his intention was. All I can say is thank you. It is very kind of you to listen to my point of view."

"I am your man, so it is my job to listen to you, even when my intention was not to bother you in our family squabbles."

"Well I am here now, I am involved. So this is what I have to say: Your family loves you. And all of you love your mom, right?"

He nodded his head in assent.

Continuing on, Olivia said, "…as a mother, perhaps one of her greatest joys is celebrating the day you were born. Though she is weakened by sickness, you are blessed to have a mother who wants to celebrate you even as a grown man. I would give anything to have my mother around to celebrate my birthdays. Let your mother have her way, whatever that looks like. I promise you, it will bring her happiness. We will all be here to ensure she does not get too tired. We did come here to support her, right?"

"You're right Olivia. Thank you for allowing me to see that the celebration will make her happy. I can do things the hard way sometimes."

She laughed. "That is an understatement Javier. And I thought you said Alberto is the bull-headed brother!"

"Yes well, he was a good teacher!"

"Perhaps too good. Remember how much you were worried about your mother back on the island. Now you have an opportunity to love her and let her spoil you. Take advantage of it."

"I will go and tell her dinner is on." He kissed Olivia on her forehead. "I'll see you upstairs." He let her go and off he went.

She sat back down on the sofa quite content. She wished she had some more of that lemonade.

Chapter 16

"Where choice begins, Paradise ends, innocence ends, for what is Paradise but the absence of any need to choose this action?" ~
Arthur Miller

Dinner the next evening seemed to go on and on. Not so much the amount of food that was served, but all of activity and the late hour of mealtime. Olivia had eaten appetizers consisting of tapas dishes which she knew to be Spanish small plates. And she had devoured the most amazing paella—a Gutierrez family recipe. All in all, it had been an amazing meal and she was not sure whether birthday cake was part of Spanish tradition or not. Something sweet would be welcome as a last course.

Looking around the table, she was amazed at the hugeness of the room. Everyone had a place at the table that with seating for eighteen. Javier's father sat at the head of the table, with his wife to his right. Then across from his mom, was Javier, as today was his birthday. She was next to him to his left. Javier had explained that normally it was Alberto who sat in that seat. On special occasions, the guest of honor always sat closest to Antonio and Catherine. Otherwise the guest would be lost amidst all the chatter and activity. No one else had assigned seating when there was a family gathering.

Stifling a yawn and not wanting to be rude, Olivia was surprised to find herself tired from watching the interactions of all the brothers and assortment of relatives. If only she had taken a siesta earlier in the day versus reading in the library, perhaps midnight would not seem so late. Cousin Eduardo had just made a toast celebrating that Javier had indeed survived to see another birthday considering his choice of careers. Javier had told her that he and Eduardo had gone together to university, and for years they had been very close. When Javier went to work in the Caribbean, they had grown apart or grown up. He hoped that Eduardo being here this evening, they could again forge a bond greater than family ties. She was excited for the opportunity for them to reconnect, and it would seem that both men wanted that too.

Next to speak was Javier's father. "Mi hijo, you honor me. As a father, I wanted only the best for you and your brothers. It would seem that in your youth, you were reckless and passionate." He paused. "I was worried that perhaps you would not survive. However, you not only survived, you learned to be an amazing pilot. And now, you use your talents, not for your own greed, but for the good of others and you risk your life to save people in need. All of us agree, that is remarkable. This year, you came home to be with Mama as she gets well, and you bought the beautiful jewel of a woman, Olivia, with you. We are proud of you. May you have many years of an amazing life to come. Happy Birthday and Cheers!"

Everyone raised their glasses, and echoed 'cheers.' Then they drank.

Javier stood with his glass in hand. "Thank you mi familia, and especially Papa and Mama. I am truly blessed to have you all in my life. I appreciate this celebration even if I do not like being the center of attention. I love you all and will continue to strive to do my best to represent our family with honor, hard work, and love. I am also grateful to Olivia for coming with me to check on Mama. She has kept me calm and focused."

Everyone clapped or clanked their glasses with spoons. Javier sat back down and kissed her on her cheek.

Olivia could only hope dessert was coming shortly. She'd eaten and drank quite a bit. She just wanted to lounge back, put her feet up and relax. If she was being honest with herself, she was anxious to give Javier his birthday gift in private. It would never due to fall asleep early even though this was technically not his birthday anymore.

Mama said "Javier I had the cook make your favorite dessert. My rice pudding. I could not prepare it for you and I supervised to ensure all the right ingredients were put in."

"Thank you Mama. You know the doctor would have said you needed to be resting."

"Yes, and I would have reminded him that I was totally relaxed and did not lift a finger in supervising."

"Okay Mama, you win!" he said as he raised his hands to give in.

"Of course I win, son. It is a special occasion. I will be fine. I will rest more tomorrow, and surgery will be the day after."

On the other side of Catherine, Juan Carlos spoke. "Mama, perhaps tomorrow you would like for Lacey and I come visit in the early afternoon."

"Yes, of course. I would like that very much. I do not understand why you prefer to stay anywhere else but here in your old bedroom."

"You know Mama, I promised Lacey I would take her to stay in the old city the very next time we were here. She likes roaming through Europe's old cities, right querida?"

Lacey spoke up. "Yes, I love the charm and romance of it all."

Olivia noticed how happy Juan Carlos and Lacey were as they smiled at each other. She thought how lucky they were to have found love. Theirs was certainly a whirlwind story. She wondered what would become of her and Javier. Ahhh, he was so sexy and gorgeous as he sat next to her in his black slacks and baby blue collared shirt. His arm gently rubbed against hers and she lost all sense of the conversations happening around her. Not able to stop herself from touching him, Olivia put her hand on Javier's thigh under the table. She felt the heat and power emanating from his strong, muscled leg. She was suddenly not tired anymore.

Javier turned and looked at her with an impish smile. Then his gaze fell to her lips. That look undid her each time and she could feel the stirring low in her pelvis. She would bet he felt the urgency in her touch too. He leaned over and kissed her cheek again in a chaste kiss and whispered into her ear. "That feels really good. Will you move your hand up a little?"

"Javier stop!" She mouthed into his cheek as she smiled back at him.

"You started this" he whispered as he put his hand over hers under the table.

Her smile intensified as she continued to ignore everyone else at the noisy table. Amidst all the children, no one was paying attention to them anyway. She whispered "I have a surprise gift for you upstairs."

"Querida, does it include unwrapping you as part of birthday present?"

"Javier, shh, someone will overhear you." She could feel the intense redness that had set into her face.

"I keep telling you that they already know I am no saint. Who could keep their hands off you? You are so beautiful, well-mannered and hot in the bedroom."

Just at that moment, Olivia heard the clanking of silverware on a glass. Not sure what was going on and hoping no one noticed what they had been doing or talking about, she moved her hand from under Javier's and off his leg. She put it back on her lap under the table.

It was Javier's father who was making the noise. "Might I get everyone's attention?"

Everyone, including red-faced Olivia, turned their attention to Antonio who sat at the head of the table. It is time to sing 'Feliz Cumpleanos.' Everyone began singing. The cook brought in a birthday cake, and of course the rice pudding, a traditional dish from Jaen. Olivia tucked in more food.

Shortly after, Mama and Papa excused themselves for the night. Music started to play and some people stayed to dance. Some of the brothers went off to smoke cigars and drink brandy.

Javier said to Olivia, "ready to go upstairs? I could use some alone time with you."

She nodded her head yes. They snuck away and no one really noticed.

Once he closed the door to their room, he pulled her into his arms and kissed her. One of those kisses that knocked the wind out of her.

"What is that for?" she said when he let her up for air.

"I have wanted to kiss you like that for hours."

"Oh!"

"Now I want to put my hand back on your thigh to finish what we started under the table."

"Ha! Patience Birthday Man! First, I have your birthday gift. And no it is not me. Well, not exactly."

"Olivia, I did not want you to give me a gift. Your presence here is gift enough."

She went over to her laptop bag and pulled out the notecard. She handed it to Javier. "Happy Birthday Javier, a little late."

He took the envelope. She watched as he opened it. He pulled out the card and read the message.

He tilted his head and looked her in the eye. "Querida, you love me? Really? Are you sure?"

She smiled. "Yes, I love you, you stubborn man. I have loved you for some time. It is hard for me to express my feelings. I did not plan it, but I cannot deny it. I am alive with you and I feel like I never have before."

"Say it again, please?"

"What?"

"Say you love me?"

"I love you Javier!"

He moved so quickly Olivia was surprised. He picked her up and twirled her around. "That is the best birthday gift I have every gotten." He let her go and she slowly slid down his body. "I love you Olivia" he said and his lips found hers again. Sealed with a kiss. She was clear that he was happy. All was well for this moment. When he stopped planting kisses all over her face and neck, he took her hands in his and led her to the bed. They made love with such intensity and passion, it scared Olivia. She'd never experienced this kind of overwhelming love with a man. *Don't think too much*, her inner voice said. *Not tonight!* Like so many nights before, they fell asleep in each other's arms.

Chapter 17

"Thousands of candles can be lighted from a single candle, and the life of the candle will not be shortened. Happiness never decreases by being shared." ~ Buddha

Time had gone by very quickly and today was surgery day. They'd been at the hospital since dawn. All the brothers were there. The entire lot of them had been silent for what seemed like eons. They sat and stared at their phones, paced or stood to lean back against the waiting room wall.

There was no sign of the antics and mischief Olivia had seen in the days leading up to now. It was their mother, their rock of life who had shown she was human and not invincible after all. Olivia knew that experience as she'd watched Jane's health decline. Thankfully, Javier's mother was not Jane and the prognosis was good.

Still, it was a sight to see, the male Gutierrez clan being 'concerned.' Lacey and Olivia were the only two females there. Olivia had attempted to stay at the house to no avail and could still hear Javier's words: 'no, I need you to go. You are level-headed and I will draw on your strength for support.' So she went. Olivia felt she did not belong here invading their private moments and it was as awkward as she had known it would be. It was difficult to watch someone you care about helpless to do anything other than pray and hope for the best.

It was also a little overwhelming watching Javier's father silently fret over his wife's condition. He just sat there in one of the gray chairs lining the back of the waiting room, his head against the wall behind him. He stared into space. The dark circles under his eyes and weariness told the tale that he'd not slept much. He'd stayed the night in her hospital room at her bedside. Olivia was convinced no greater real-life love story existed than between Javier's parents, Mama G and Papa G, as she'd now labeled them. They genuinely loved one another. His heartbreak showed in the look of being lost with no direction or purpose.

The names Mama G and Papa G sounded like Javier's folks were the heads of a mafia family—people who ran the world. Nothing to base it on other than Olivia had her own secret nicknames for most people. It helped her gain perspective with her thoughts as her mind was always racing. Plus, she had to refer to them by something. Calling them by their first names was a ridiculous proposition. Olivia didn't think that way, and she'd also been raised to respect elders. She couldn't conform to calling them by their first names even at the request of his parents and their constant correction she stop making them feel old using Mr. and Mrs. Gutierrez. They were such nice people and Olivia was glad she'd come home with Javier to meet them.

Mama G had arrived at the hospital late last night, as agreed. In preparing to leave the palazzo, she had given hugs to all her sons and Lacey before coming to stand before her last. Olivia touched her skin remembering how Mama G had gently rubbed both her cheeks with her warm hands. She'd said, "it has been a pleasure to meet you dearest Olivia. I like you. You are good for my son. Please do stay until I return. The run of this house is yours." Then she smiled and hugged me. Olivia felt loved.

Mama G let her go, walked over to pick up her purse and made her way to the big entry doorway that made her five foot, eight inch frame look like a dwarf. She turned back to face all of us assembled, put up a hand, waved and said 'goodbye.' Her last statement as we watched her leave the living room was "don't any of you worry. I am not dying before you all create my grandbabies. If you want to help me along, stop worrying prematurely, and get to work procreating!"

Papa G scoffed at his wife as he held the door for her. "They are already worried enough about you, and you keep up the pressure to make babies."

She turned to face her husband. "Ha! If they really loved me, they'd give me the one thing I want in my old age, babies to spoil and love."

Olivia had looked around the room. All the men were wide-eyed with dismay. No one said anything, including Papa G. Mama had spoken and they had their marching orders.

As soon as the door closed, everyone disappeared in quiet silence. She suspected in addition to worrying about mama and making babies, they were thinking the night would be short as they all planned to be at the hospital in the morning to await Mama G's successful surgery.

And now here they were and here Olivia sat, wondering if this would all work out okay. They were in the best hospital money could buy and while Barcelona was not just around the corner, they were close enough to home to ground them to their Jaen roots. But was it enough to save Mama G's life? She hoped so. This family would be devastated if their mama got sicker or worse.

The doctor appeared and interrupted Olivia's rambling thoughts. Papa G went to stand in front of him. Javier stood up, and she followed to stand by his side. The doctor began by shaking Papa G's hand, then he smiled and started speaking in rapid fire Spanish. Javier pulled her close to him and interpreted for her in quiet tones. "He said the surgery was a success; she'd been a fighter; they'd repaired the valves around her heart and removed the blockages. They could expect a full recovery and for her age that was the best possible outcome. The doctor says she is sedated and resting back in her room now." Olivia watched as they all sighed in relief, including her. It's as if no one had breathed in the hours they'd waited and now they could.

Papa G asked if he could see her. The doctor said 'yes they all could, but only for a short time as she needs to remain quiet.' After he left the room, they all gathered in a circle. They held hands and prayed a short prayer of thanksgiving and blessing. At least that was what Olivia could make out in their foreign tongue.

The sons agreed to only a couple minutes visit in order to kiss their Mama, and then they'd go back home. They'd leave Papa G to stay with his wife for the first shift.

Lacey and Olivia both said they'd stay in the waiting room not wanting to tire Mama G. Thirty minutes later and she and Javier were leaving the hospital. He looked tired, yet relieved. Olivia was grateful she had been there for him.

Once in the car, he turned to her. He reached over and pushed an errant curl behind my ear. "Thank you querida for being here."

"You're welcome. I'm so glad the surgery went well and your mom will be good as new."

"Me too. She's a tough old cookie who will heal fast. And we all know she's serious about not dying before she has 'grand babies,' emphasis on more than one. The baby Marcelo is expecting does not get us off the hook."

Olivia laughed. "Well I guess Juan Carlos and Lacey better get busy!"

"Yes, since most of us aren't married, Mama can't say too much. She is very religious and doesn't advocate children outside marriage. She will play Cupid on steroids if we don't watch her."

"She seems so progressive yet you imply she's old fashioned and conservative. She doesn't seem to mind us staying in the same bed under her roof."

Javier said, "she is practical knowing her sons are not saints. More than anything she wants us under her roof, where she can watch us like hawks. What time we come in, sober or drunk. Who came home with us. What we ate and how much. We are used to it, it's the way she loves us."

"She's not there now though. I am sure she is not comfortable not knowing."

"You best believe she has Papa and spies that report in on all that goes on at the estate."

"I'll remember that," she said as she continued to wring her hands as they sat in her lap.

He reached over and squeezed her hands. "No worries my Olivia. She has taken a liking to you and you have nothing to concern your beautiful mind with. Today is a good day!"

"Yes, it is." She smiled brightly at him.

"Now let's go." He said as he turned his attention to the steering wheel and shifting the car into gear. Then he looked over to her. "I'm sleepy. I want to go home, eat and relax. When we get back to the palazzo, I hope to entice you to take a siesta with me." He winked his eye at her.

With as much of a straight face as she could manage, she said "I can't believe you are flirting with me Mr. Gutierrez."

He laughed a hearty laugh. "Oh querida! You know I am and plan to make good on my words. Just you wait till I get you back home."

Olivia giggled, leaned back in the Italian leather seats and said nothing more. She couldn't wait!

Chapter 18

"I love her and that's the beginning and end of everything."
~ F. Scott Fitzgerald

Two Weeks Later

Something always came along to alter his plans. The call he had just received was no different. Now he had to locate Olivia and convince her to stay here until he returned. He knew his parents would not mind her staying. He could see they took to her and would expect her to be here while he went off to work. Duty called, and he was needed. He hoped to return within a week, and with search and rescue, no one knew the exact timing of coming home. His parents understood his job and what it required. Now that Mama was expected to fully recover, and was home recuperating, he would not feel guilty for having to leave her.

Olivia was a different story. He was thrilled Olivia had revealed that she loved him. The sex was amazing and the moments they'd shared left him wondering how he had any good times in life before she showed up. Yet he still sensed she was holding back from giving all of herself to him. He was frustrated and unsure of how to convince her that he loved her, and was not going anywhere. Hell, if truth be told, he was not going to let her go. If she stayed here, perhaps she would learn to trust him. He knew he had found the woman to be his wife, his soul mate. And he was sure if he proposed to her, she would bolt like an untrained colt. The timing had to be just right. He thought to himself, one precious step at a time. He would get what he wanted.

Javier found Olivia in the gardens outside the formal library. He suspected it was one of her favorite places in the whole of the estate. In the back corner on the other side of the hedge is a fountain and small pool amidst trellised lattices that connected plants, blossoms and vines to the high-backed walls. The 'beautiful flowers of Spain,' as Mama had named them, and a few from other exotic locations were in full bloom. The fragrances were so heady and full of life that he was unsure how Olivia could be productive there without being distracted. Honeysuckle, roses, and the scent of lavender were his mother's favorites. So few ever came here unless there was a formal garden party happening or his parents went on what they liked to call a 'a picnic close to home.' With his mom recovering from surgery, he knew his father would not stray far beyond their wing of the palazzo.

Javier recalled that this used to be his refuge. He'd come here to escape and found it easy to hide, daydream and pretend he was somewhere else in the world. There was a view of the mountains that Mama loved. Mama's parents, Santos and Catalina grew up in Jaen and fell in love. From two different families, they were ironically meant to be together, like his mama and papa, and just like he was convinced that he and Olivia were destined to stay together. Abuela Catalina was named after the mountain range Santa Catalina. When her parents had their only child, a daughter, of course they named her Catherine after her mother, which is another variation of Catalina. He loved the traditions of his family and even though he had not told Olivia about it, she seemed drawn to this place. She had mentioned that she liked the solitude when it came time to write; the perfect place to create. This was also the perfect place to talk, to get his way.

She was curled up on one of the stone benches typing away on her iPad. He came to stop right in front of her. She looked up as his shadow crossed her light. She fixed dazzling blue eyes upon him with a look that would bring a lesser man to his knees and beg to stare.

"Yes" she spoke on a breathy sigh.

Oh, those are the exact words he wanted to hear. He promised himself that no matter what she was embroiled in with her writing, he would figure out how to be making love to her pronto. He was not leaving Spain without again touching her entire body, caressing every curve, moving inside her. Otherwise, he would be a mess out there. He was determined to give her something to long for just like he longed to be with her. Better get the inevitable over first.

"I have to return to work. There is a missing boat that I need to help search for with my unique expertise. It is a research ship that disappeared off radar, and it is carrying some of the world's most renowned scientists."

"Oh? I will begin packing at once."

"No! I want you to stay here querida. I do not know exactly how long I will be gone. No more than a week I believe. I had hoped you would stay here with my family, and be here when I come back."

A pensive look came across her features. "Javier haven't we been through this before? Last time, I gave in to you."

"Do you regret coming here to spend time with me, meet my family, see where I grew up, and those things that are important to me?"

"No, and this is different."

"It is no different. You do not have to leave. Mi casa et su casa."

She lowered her head, and Javier did not know what was going on in her pretty little head. She sat there in the middle of the garden looking down at her hands as she twisted them in her lap. She bit her lip and he knew she wanted to say something.

"Olivia, look at me." She looked up tentatively, and then looked back down to her lap.

"Please, Olivia. I want nothing more than to push you against that tree, kiss you really hard, and take you right here for anyone to see."

She looked up at him shocked by his statement.

"Do I have your attention now?"

"Yes, you have my attention!"

"Good. I am working and I want you to stay here with my parents for a couple of weeks. It would mean a lot to me knowing you are here at the palazzo where you are taken care of."

"Javier, you cannot keep expecting me to stay or come when you tell me."

He smiled at the double meaning. And he was going to make sure she did come for him very soon. "Okay go with me then back to the Caribbean. We can then return here to check on Mama when this mission is complete."

"When do you have to leave?"

"In six hours. There is a search underway, and if they are not found by tomorrow morning, we will start at daybreak in their time zone."

"I don't understand. Javier, what you are asking of me is not fair. You want me to choose in one moment and I do not know how to do that."

Lowering his body to kneel in front of her, he said, "querida it is simple, no? Just say yes."

She looked deep into his eyes, and melted. He leaned in and kissed her. Before long, he had carried her into the palazzo and up to his bedroom and made good on his earlier promise. He was sure he had yet to get an answer, and perhaps she might be persuaded in other ways.

Javier dressed as Olivia watched. He had descended from the shower and she was unsure of what to say. After a couple of hours making love and a quick nap, she was emotionally exhausted. She did not want to leave the palazzo so abruptly. That was rude. And she did not feel it was her place to stay here without him. Torn in so many directions.

"Olivia, please don't make me leave here without your answer" he said as he sat down next to her on the bed.

He spoke and it was time for her to make a decision. "Javier, I will stay here for a week."

Stay? Javier was desperate for a long-term commitment from Olivia as he no longer thought what they had

226

would fade. She was his ending and beginning, and he wouldn't lose her.

"Querida, I know I have to go, and this is going to sound strange considering I am getting on a plane to disappear for a few days: I've been thinking we should always be together."

"What are you talking about Javier?"

"I am not very romantic so I'm sure there's a better way to do this." He sighed and got down on his knees before her. He rubbed his finger across her cheek and placed a simple and chaste kiss on her lips. Olivia always felt her eyes flutter shut when her kissed her. When she opened her eyes, he was staring deeply into hers, the depth of his stare boring a hole through her as if he were looking into her soul. "Marry me Olivia? Let's create a forever paradise with each other. We have love to carry us through anything. I want you to be my wife."

"What did you say?" She could not trust she was hearing him correctly. She shook her head to lift her mind from the daze. "Did you just ask me to marry you?"

She watched him run his hand through his hair.

"Yes, even though I am sure from your response I am not doing it right." He took her hands into his and interlaced their fingers. "Look, we are good together. Making love with you is like flying to new heights, and I

227

could listen to you talk all day. We enjoy being around each other, we both love family. You even boss me around and I listen, mostly. That has to be a sign that we are meant to marry. I want you to have faith in what we have."

"Javier, I do. Sort of. I get that I have doubts about how any of this happened or how it could possibly work out. And I love you. I do. But marriage is a serious commitment, way different than just being in the same place."

"I know Olivia. Trust me. I know what I want. I want you, our marriage and our forever together."

"But"...she was about to continue her protest when he placed a finger across her lips.

"Shhhhhh. Olivia, just consider my proposal. It is all I ask for now." And then he leaned in and kissed her. She could not resist him. In spite of her shock at his proposal, all thought ceased when they kissed. She put her arms around his neck and pressed her body to his kneeling figure.

When they emerged for air, Olivia quietly whispered. "I will consider it."

"Thank you querida. As much as I want to go back to bed with you, I must go now. I love you. I will return back here to your arms as soon as my mission ends. It's my promise."

She nodded. "Goodbye" she said quietly.

She watched as he rose from the floor. He was such a giant amongst men. She thought it best to say no more. She could already feel the war ripping through her body and the tears threatening just below the surface. She'd almost bought into his fantasy and acquiesced to say yes. Almost...

Don't you dare cry she commanded her mind. *Let him go. He already told you he's coming back for you.* Why was she being emotional anyway?

Olivia never expected a marriage proposal from the wayward Pilot. He had to be out of his mind. Even if she could believe what he said, how would she ever survive his working lifestyle. She suspected he preferred working over everything else. Every time he left, she'd cry herself to sleep, wondering why he'd left her, if he had gotten lost at sea or used work as an excuse to be away from her. Would he use it as an opportunity to go be with other women? Would he cheat on me? Would he die at work?

She sighed. Olivia, stop the madness. He's gone for now. You have some time to think, build your resolve and practice telling him no. This is not a fairytale. You already fell in love with him. That is quite enough!

Olivia felt a tear escape her eyelid. As it slowly ran down her face, she swiped it away. *You do not need a man to tell you anything Olivia Stevenson! When he comes back, you give him a big, fat NO!*

Chapter 19

"Every love story is beautiful but ours is my favorite."
~ Anonymous

Olivia had been diligently trying to work since Javier left. She was committed to channeling her missing him into her work. He had been gone for four days and three long nights. Still she'd muddled through. Right now she was in the garden listening to the fountain bubble. It was almost dusk in the evening. September days in Jaen started out hot, and temperatures decreased as the night called forth the darkness. Dinner was not usually until around 9:30 pm to allow for the day's heat to decline and the work in the fields to be done.

Her phone buzzed on her lap. It was the Pilot. "Querida?"

"Hey there you. I was worried. How's the search going?"

"We found them. They survived. However, now we are trying to find pieces of their ship that carried their research. The weather has not really been cooperating. I am sorry for not calling sooner. Where we are is very remote."

"Not a problem as long as you are okay."

"Yes, I am fine. I miss seeing you. I miss having you in my arms."

"I miss you too."

"How's Mama?"

"She's doing great. The doctor says she is on track and he is pleased with her progress. Your father hovers around her very closely."

"Good, give them my love."

"I will. They will be excited to hear you called. They say you often do not call when you are away."

"Yes, I wanted to hear your voice. What have you been doing?"

"Actually I have been working and spending time with your family. You are so lucky to have a great family. They actually look like they enjoy one another's company."

"Yes, we're close and take for granted that everyone does not enjoy spending time around their siblings. I am pleased they have included you."

She laughed. "Yes, they definitely included me in their antics and mischief."

"Perfecto! Querida, I have to go now. I love you. I will be back to you as soon as I can."

"I love you back Javier. Stay safe and come home soon."

The line went dead. Olivia sighed. At least now she knew he was okay. She closed her laptop, gathered her papers and went into the house to deliver news of Javier's message.

Chapter 20

*"If we could make our house a home, and then make it a sanctuary,
I think we could truly find paradise on Earth."*
~ Alexandra Stoddard

Olivia was in the window seat of Javier's bedroom, leaned back with her feet up, and staring out at the olive groves that peppered the distance for as far as one could see. She briefly looked down at her computer sitting open on her lap. The word processing application gave off a bright glare of white, and the cursor was blinking at her every second...blink...blink...blink. Here I go again, daydreaming about him. "Do you ever get anything done Olivia?" she asked herself out loud. She sighed and looked out the window once more. She thought back to last night when Javier surprised her by making a grand appearance in their bedroom to say 'I'm back.' He pulled her from the bed where she was reading in the lamplight and coaxed her into the shower with him. It was amazing what he could illicit her to do with just one passionate kiss. The thought of that homecoming celebration made her blush. That man is so....

Get a grip Olivia. This isn't like some Cinderella fairy tale. It can't last! His marriage proposal can't be real. Javier already told you he had nothing to offer you, and now he offers you everything. He comes and goes on his own schedule. Well, at least it seems like he does! A few hours ago, he went to meet up with his brothers to let them know he was officially back for now, and here you sit pretending to work. Who knows how long it will be before he is called back to duty...He's unpredictable! He's dangerous!

As if on cue, the door opened and Olivia turned from the window to see Javier sweep into their suite of rooms like a ball of adrenaline. She squinted to see what he was holding in his hand. Looked to be an oversized envelope.

"Hello querida! Did you miss me?" he said as he came over and placed a kiss on her right cheek, then her left. Then he stepped back a few feet.

What is he up to? Olivia smiled and accepted his customary kiss of greeting. "Yes, of course I did. I always miss you. What's that you are carrying?" She gestured to the large envelope he held in his hands.

He looked down and then held up the envelope. "This? This is an invitation for us to attend the company's ball this Friday night."

"No, I'm not interested!" Olivia said looking down to save her work and then removing her computer from her lap. She knew they were about to have a discussion. One she was dreading.

He ran his free hand through his hair. "Look, I know I got back from my mission late last evening, and it would be great if we could go hide out to catch up, only the two of us. You know as well as I that ain't happening because you aren't going to agree to us leaving Mama. So let's just go to the ball and have a few carefree hours querida."

Olivia wanted to give in, do the things normal couples did. Pretend it was a fun date out with Javier. She knew better. She didn't like that he reappeared and made demands of her, not respecting the value of her time. He played with her when it suited him. "No, I don't want to go to a ball. I came here with you to check on your mom. Under duress I might add!"

"Yes, I know. But Mama is going to make an appearance. She made the request I bring you. She even said she would love to see us there, dancing and having a good time like normal couples."

Using his mother's exact words weakened her defenses. "You are an impossible man! I do not want to disappoint your mother, at least not right now."

"Really? Me impossible? It's not possible. I make requests querida. Don't shoot me, I am just the messenger."

"If not for your mother and her frailty I probably would shoot you!"

He came over to stand in front of her. Olivia was being pouty, and she knew it. He put his right index finger under her chin and lifted it so she was forced to look into his gaze. "Keeping Mama calm and happy is only part of my desire to go. I want to see you all dressed up and on my arm. Then when we get back here, it will be my great pleasure to unwrap you like the gift you are to my life."

Olivia heard him sigh as if longing for more right this moment. She was afraid he might bring up his marriage proposal, but he did not. Instead she let her eyes close as he reached out to pull her up into his arms. He captured her lips in a gentle kiss meant to unnerve her resolve. It worked. She was about to melt when he broke off their kiss.

He held her away from him, still keeping her in his outstretched arms. He looked into her eyes and asked, "it's settled then, no? You will be my date?"

"Yes, I will. However, I did not plan to go out to a formal event while here. I have nothing to wear. I need to go shopping."

"I figured as much. Juan Carlos said Lacey too mentioned she had nothing to wear. Would you like to go on a shopping expedition, just you women?"

"Yes, I definitely do not want to shop with you."

"What? You do not want to model dresses and undergarments for me. I would be an avid watcher!"

"I bet you would," she laughed out loud. "No thank you! Spare me the premature observation... I will prefer to go with Lacey."

"Very good querida, I will arrange it for tomorrow. I am a patient man, and time is on my side. It will not be long before I see you in your beautiful dress and what is under it as well."

Olivia chuckled..."yes, you are perhaps right."

******

The next morning after breakfast, Lacey was scheduled to meet Olivia at the front door of the palazzo at half past nine. Javier had gone off to help his papa before sunrise. She didn't go back to sleep after he'd left as she loved to shop. Instead she'd stayed awake and looked through some fashion magazines to contemplate her look for the party. She needed dramatic, yet understated.

Shopping was always a wonderful treat, even if she didn't buy anything. She could never quite find the right words to describe the feeling of retail therapy. It was like having chicken soup without being sick or stopping to smell the roses even if it was not the first days of Spring. And as long as she could keep doing it, who cared.

She arrived downstairs just as Juan Carlos was standing in the open doorway handing off the keys to one of his classy sedans to Lacey. Actually, she'd caught them being kissy face as if no one was expected.

"Sorry to interrupt you two love birds?"

Juan Carlos stopped kissing his wife, but did not take his eyes from her. "No interruption, just a pause." Lacey stared back at him and Olivia could see she got some message just between the two of them. Lacey gently placed her hand against his cheek. "It's a promise, so don't go disappearing into work if you are going to make good on your word."

He laughed and said "woman, you are sweet temptation to the honey bee stuck in your nectar! I'll be here waiting." He then turned and began to walk toward the steps passing by Olivia as she stood on the last one. He added "you two have a great time shopping. And Olivia, please don't keep my honey out all day."

I giggled from his silliness. "We will I chimed in." I was even more convinced as I watched those two that true love and romance really does exist.

Lacey jangled the keys! "Don't mind him. Ready for our wild shopping adventure? We have one quick pickup to make and then we'll hit the best boutiques."

Off they went for a day of shopping! The stop they had to make was to pick up Arabella, Chief Scientist for the family company. She was already at the office, a true workaholic. Turns out all three ladies were in need of dress attire for the gala.

True to her word, Lacey took them to all the best stores and each of them found the perfect ensemble. They named themselves, '*Tres Hermanas*,' as by the end of lunch it seemed like they were related and could have grown up together. Lacey the wild adventurer, Arabella the nerdy and studious one and Olivia, the hopeless romantic. Olivia had laughed harder than she ever remembered. No matter what, they were going to be lifelong friends going forward.

With everything they needed in hand, Lacey dropped Arabella back at the office, and then she and Olivia returned back to the estate. They'd made plans to meet back up midday Friday for spa and makeup before getting dressed to go. Olivia was especially pleased she'd convinced Arabella to explore her femininity. This ball was going to be memorable, and just maybe Arabella would break out of her shell and go out more.

Olivia thanked Lacey for a great time, and reminded her to go find Juan Carlos so he would not die without his honey. Lacey rolled her eyes and yet they both knew she was indeed going to go find her husband.

Olivia dragged herself and packages up the endless front staircase.

She opened the door to her rooms, exhausted and wanting a siesta. Walking in she saw Javier sitting in the chair, his feet up on the ottoman reading the newspaper. She never tired of looking at him. Dressed in casual slacks and a pale rose colored, button down shirt that was open at the collar, and with shirt sleeves rolled back to his elbows. The outline of his olive skin and flexed muscles always peeking through whatever shirt he wore. She wanted to trail her hands down the front and help him out of it.

He cleared his throat. Olivia looked up slowly and smiled. He knew what she was imagining. "Let me help you with your packages he said as he started to get up. How was your shopping expedition Olivia?"

"Oh no, it's fine. You stay there. Shopping was eventful and really enjoyable!" Olivia said as she laid her packages down and went into the closet to hang up the dress bag. She didn't want to show him her purchases until she donned them Friday night. She went on, "I like being around Lacey and she brought along Arabella."

"Oh, our new Chief Scientist?" he asked.

"Yes, the one and only" Olivia chimed in as she reappeared in the bedroom. She skipped over and gave Javier a quick peck on the lips, then went and plopped down on the couch across from him. She pushed her low heels off and put her feet up, continuing to speak. "Arabella too needed something to wear for the ball. She calls herself a geek who has no time for these kind of 'foo foo' events. She also confessed she loves what she's doing and has often worked eighteen hour days since arriving here in Jaen. I don't envy her."

Javier chuckled. He put his newspaper down on the table, moved from his chair to the couch, and lifted her feet to slide in under them. He started rubbing her tired and aching soles. "Hmmm that feels amazing."

"I aim to please. I did not mean to interrupt your story. Do continue."

Olivia did as he asked. "Thanks to me though she will be 'va va va voom' and turn every head at that party. This event is the perfect time for her to make her grand debut!"

"Ah, it sounds like you women are up to some scheming. I guess now you are excited to go?"

"No scheming. Arabella is a beautiful woman with a prime role in your family's dynasty. There is no reason for her to be mousy and hide behind her test tubes and scientific manuals all the time. Plus, every ball deserves a Cinderella! I helped her pick out a great dress, suited to her curvaceous body and those fiery red curls. She has really great hair! So to answer your question yes, I want to be there to see her having the good time she has earned."

"Ahhhh I fell in love with a hopeless romantic! I love it! Alberto better watch out or else he's going to have unwanted competition. That will be fun to watch."

Olivia tilted her head. "You brother Alberto? He wants Arabella? Really!"

"Let's just say according to the rumor mill, when those two are around sparks fly and everyone runs the opposite way to avoid getting burned. Alberto is a proud and angry man. He was not pleased the Board replaced him with Arabella, bringing her from America, and giving her carte blanche to implement a new extraction process for the olives. He considers her an outsider and hates her, supposedly! Mama is convinced they will end up together. But she is a hopeless romantic too!"

"This will be interesting to see. Maybe it will inspire a new book for me to write."

"Now, now my little vixen, you already have your hands full with me. Don't forget you promised me dancing and your undivided attention."

"Ha, I did not. If memory serves me correctly, you promised your mother we'd dance the night away." She smiled. "I simply agreed to buy a dress and go."

"Touché querida. Will you model your purchases for me?"

"Absolutely not, patient man! You'll have to wait like the rest of the Gutierrez brothers."

"Fine, don't blame me for trying to practice unwrapping you from the dress a little early. Since you won't show me, it seems like we have time for a siesta before dinner. He lifted one of her feet and kissed her toe."

The caress was enough to send a jolt of heat to her core. "I think a siesta is exactly the medicine I need to rejuvenate my exhausted body."

"Shall we?" He said as he began planting kisses up her leg.

"Oh yes!" she said through the fog of sensations.

He moved from under her and scooped her into his arms. She began to giggle as he tickled her neck with his tongue. "You are such a self-sacrificing savior" she said. And off to bed they went.

Chapter 21

"Every moment of our life we have an opportunity to choose joy. It is in the choice that our true freedom lies, and that freedom is, in the final analysis, the freedom to love." ~ Henri J.M Nouwen

On Friday, at a quarter past six in the evening, Olivia descended the steps in strappy sandals and a forest green, floor length gown with lace overlay. She loved the way the dress hugged her figure with its square, sleeveless bodice and mermaid flair skirt, the satin, a second skin hidden beneath the dual layers of fabric. The most striking part of the ensemble was the low cut, open back with scalloped design that framed the edges.

The team of stylists Lacey had employed to help the ladies get ready had done a great job. Olivia knew it was an illusion, far from who she normally was. Understated, yet elegant! She'd pushed Arabella to be the vixen of the night; Lacey to be the seductress. They laughed and noted she was not going to escape—thus, she was adorned the temptress. Each of them just wanting to have a few carefree hours. Arabella had gone home to get dressed and Lacey had said they would not be there at the start.

Back on the stairs, Olivia now refocused on her walking in these killer heels. She sported an upsweep hairdo, held in place by an elegant crystal clip and a few strategically placed pins. The artists, or miracle workers, as she liked to refer to them had applied flawless soft tones of makeup and a rosy gloss to her lips. She had to remember not to bite her lips tonight. The message she conveyed: 'look, don't touch.' She couldn't lie...

She felt sexy, like a femme fatale dressed to slay. And there was only one man's attention she wanted. Javier. She'd been thinking about him nonstop all day. He made her want to dress up for him. Actually he also made her want to take everything off for him too. Sometimes she wondered why she even bothered getting dressed when he was around because it wasn't long before she was out of whatever outfit she had on.

Olivia reached the landing, the halfway point of the massive staircase. She paused at the banister to steady her footing. Like clockwork, Javier appeared. He was dressed in black slacks, crisp white tuxedo shirt, freshly starched and accented with the classic black bow tie. Oh, so debonair he is. She could faint just at the mere sight of him. He was talking in Spanish on the phone; and sounded very patient even though he was giving orders of such. He must have sensed she was there as he looked up at that moment, and their eyes met. They were like two embers smoldering hot almost to flames. He stopped midstride. Then he said 'Buenas' and clicked off his phone as if she were the most important person in his world.

"You're early querida" he said. And then he began his thorough perusal. From top to bottom he studied every inch of her. She felt like a Petri dish underneath a microscopic lens.

"Dios, you look irresistible. Come, I want to see you up close." He held out his hand and her feet propelled her forward as if she were in some type of trance. She hoped she would not tumble down the steps in her ridiculously high heels, and she knew he'd catch her if she did. The look of pure lust he was giving her was making her hot and bothered already. If she wasn't concentrating so hard on gracefully walking she would be using her free hand to fan herself.

When she got to the bottom, he said in a husky voice "Turn around, I want to see all of you."

She slowly turned. When her back was fully to him, she heard his sharp intake of breath. "Stop!" She froze. She felt him approach her as she held herself still not sure her legs would hold her up for much longer. He ran his finger down the middle of her back in a slow pace. "Oh my querida...this dress is scandalous," he said in a breathy whisper. She could feel he was almost close enough to her to plaster his body against hers.

"You think it's inappropriate?"

"Oh no, it's amazing. Maybe I don't want to go to the party anymore. I want to stay here with you so you can strip for me. I already know you have nothing on underneath it but perhaps a few scraps of fabric if I'm unlucky."

With his blatant assertion, she blushed enough for her cheeks to match the red color of her lip gloss. She noticed her breathing was heavy and labored. She slowly turned around to face him. With all the composure and focus she could muster, she took a deep breath. "Too bad, we're going!" she said. "I will not disappoint your mother. And after all this hoopla to look perfect, we'll have to save the striptease till later."

Javier closed his eyes, lowered his head and rubbed his hand across his face a couple of times. He gave her a quick peck on the lips. "You win, for now. Let me get my jacket and we can go." He turned and walked away.

One crisis averted Olivia said to herself. If he'd really wanted to stay home, she would have given in. She had already seen Lacey and Arabella all made up before they parted to get dressed. They'd agreed to have a fun night with no stress.

"Ready, querida?" Javier said when he returned all dressed.

Plastering a smile on her face, Olivia threw caution to the wind and walked out the front door he'd opened for her.

"By the way, you might hear my extended family call me Ace. It's an American nickname my cousins gave me in my youth when I kept talking about being a pilot. It started out as a few jokes they'd make saying I wanted to be a bird. They'd laugh and make sounds and gestures. Every time they saw me they began mercilessly teasing me. In the end, they were the ones who looked foolish."

"Kids can be so cruel."

"Oh having as many brothers as I do, we are accustomed to someone being teased all the time. Mama forbid anyone calling me Ace in her presence. She said she and Papa named me and we didn't need nicknames messing up their creativity. As I grew older, I just accepted it and stopped making a big deal about what people say. I am grateful to my siblings and cousins for teaching me a valuable lesson early on."

"Wow, you have an amazing outlook on this. I'm not sure I'd be as gracious and forgiving."

"Boys being boys! There's nothing to forgive. I am a good pilot and they know it."

The rest of the evening went by in a blur. Javier seemed at times to think she was the center of attention and at others he acted aloof and distant. He was brooding or distracted, she couldn't tell. They definitely danced most of the night away together, with the few exceptions of talking or dancing with a cousin or two while Javier tended to business.

The Gutierrez family was huge. Javier introduced her to everyone—aunts, uncles, cousins. This is Tio or Tia or Primo. She wasn't sure if everyone was being nice because she was with 'Ace' or genuinely open and happy she was there. And unfortunately, she'd already forgotten most of their names. Nowhere in his introduction of her was a mention of his marriage proposal or a profession of love; yet with each intro he did say meet my Olivia and pulled her close to make no mistake that they were 'together.' Men are very territorial creatures. Olivia already knew that from her observations and research over time. She didn't understand it, and she suspected she never would.

This group knows how to throw and enjoy a party. Even though Olivia had no experience with big families it had been fun being around them. Since Jane's death, she'd been a loner, never quite wanting to risk that kind of heartbreak on casual friendships.

She'd had a good time at the ball even though she had not yet adjusted to the late night partying in Spain. All Olivia wanted to do now was to relax and let her hair down. Javier must have sensed that she was getting tired as shortly after she had the thought, he appeared at her side.

"Bella, you ready to go home?"

"Yes, please."

"Let's go. If we sneak away, no one will notice."

"Lovely, as I just want to take off this dress and let my hair down."

"Ah querida, it will be my pleasure to assist you. You will not have to lift a finger"

"Gee my very own knight in shining armor!" She smiled as she knew where they would end up, and she was looking forward to it.

"But of course!" He kissed her forehead, slipped his arm around her waist and led her toward the door.

******

They awoke the next morning to the Javier's cell phone buzzing on the table. He reached across her body and picked it up. "Hello."

She was still half asleep, but she felt the covers move as he sat up.

"Yes, I understand. I will be there in ten hours."

She knew what that meant. He was being called to duty. She was starting to notice a pattern that would follow him around the world. Well, she knew what his career was about before she ever slept with him, let alone fell in love.

251

He hung up the phone and placed it on the bed next to him. He then turned to face her. She decided to speak up first. "I heard. You have to go."

"Good morning querida" he said as he pulled her into his embrace. "Yes, as much as I do not want to, I have to go. A hurricane might turn and enter the Caribbean Sea in the next three days and we have to prepare for any possible rescues."

"Okay. Well before you ask, I am not trying to have a repeat discussion. You will go, stay safe and I will see you when you get back."

"Thank you for understanding. I promise to come back as soon as I can, querida. Even though I am not in your presence, if my heart is beating, then you and I are connected. You have my heart. Listen to it now? Hear it beat for you?" She put her hand over his chest. She leaned her head against her hand and they were silent. With that declaration, she lifted her head and kissed him.

Breaking off their kiss, he said, "Olivia, look at me? You have my word to you to always love you. I honor my word, live from my word."

They made love and she did everything she could to hold it together and live in this moment.

Chapter 22

*"A woman is like a tea bag - you can't tell how strong she is until
you put her in hot water." ~ Eleanor Roosevelt*

Time to go mope in my room! Olivia said out loud as
she massaged her aching scalp with her left hand. She
was tired of missing Javier who had been gone for days.
She had a headache in the back of her head that radiated
down her neck. The medicine she had taken with lunch
was not working. Maybe a little nap will ease this
tension and stop the throbbing, she thought as she got up
and headed toward the palazzo.

Fifty steps and Olivia reached one of the many entrances
off the massive garden, the library. She liked walking
through the library as it was the quickest way to the back
staircase and it led to his suite. Rarely anyone used those
stairs to go up to the second level. It was a perfect
escape that would keep her unseen.

Olivia opened the French doors and walked forward.
Once inside, she pushed the doors shut behind her and
leaned against them. Immediately she noticed the cool
temperature in the room. Thank goodness for air
conditioning, she sighed and closed her eyes for a
moment. Deep breath, exhale! Again. Deep breath,
exhale. Exerting the least amount of energy she could,
she opened her eyes and walked across the room
oblivious to every book she still wanted to read.

"Come dearest Olivia, sit for a few minutes and have some tea with me?" She heard a familiar voice say.

Olivia stopped abruptly mid-stride, almost jumping out of her skin. It was Javier's mom, who was sitting in one of the wingback armchairs in the corner.

"Oh hi Mrs. Gutierrez. I was just passing through taking the shortest way back to my room."

"You do not look well. And I told you, call me Mama. Anyway, come sit," she said soothingly and gestured to the matching chair and ottoman next to hers.

Olivia slowly padded her way to the matching chair. Her head was throbbing now more than ever. "Mrs. Gutierrez, I mean Mama, I have a headache and was going to lie down."

"Well, have a cup of tea. I promise it will make it better. I often get migraine headaches. My holistic doctor says I should drink chamomile and green tea."

"I'm not much of a tea drinker." Olivia said desperately.

"Yes, well there is always coffee, juice or water. You may have whatever you like. Come, I want to see why you are looking miserable and ask your opinion while Javier is not underfoot."

Wary of what opinion Olivia could give, she knew Mama G was making a statement not a request. She watched the woman pour steaming hot water into an empty cup and over a freshly laden tea bag. Olivia winched at the throbbing pain in her head, but she forced herself to focus. Two cups, one waiting for her arrival. This could not be a coincidence.

Mama G handed the cup to Olivia and with a dainty smile Olivia accepted. "Thank you" she said as she blew on the cup's contents. As she looked up from the cup she asked, "What did you want to discuss?"

"I think Javier should settle down."

Olivia had just taken a small sip of the hot liquid and almost spit it out. Javier was right when he said his mother would ensure her sons moved forward. She'd have to be careful not to say much. She leaned forward and set the cup down. Then she cleared her throat. "Mama, why are you seeking my opinion on this instead of taking it up with Javier?"

"I think the decision is up to you, not him. We all see how he looks at you. It warms my heart that he loves you. He will do whatever you want. If you want to settle down, he will. I believe you are the perfect woman for him. "

"I don't feel comfortable talking with you about this."

"Olivia, I promise to just listen. It is not my place to tell you how to live your life. I would hate for Javier to mess up the good thing he has with you. There is obviously something wrong."

"I just haven't been sleeping well since he left. I miss him. I am grateful that he has a career doing something he loves."

"That is understandable."

"Thank you for asking and understanding. I am sure in a few days I will be good as new. With you recovering from surgery, there is no reason to fret over my mild illness."

Olivia was not going to say any more. She did not want Mama G to know that Javier had proposed, and she was not sure she could accept. That would put other people into their personal business. She was unwilling to do that. She'd figure it out.

"Olivia, I just wanted you to know where I stand."

"I am sure that whatever is meant to be with Javier and I, it will get sorted out. Enough about me. How are you?"

"Very kind of you to ask. I am well. The road to recovery is slow, but I am headed in the right direction."

"Might I ask you something?"

"Anything, querida."

"Would you tell me about the city of Jaen?"

"Of course."

Olivia listened as Mama G told her about the town, it's cathedral and quaint village setting. Mama suggested she go and explore—see it for oneself. Olivia decided to go explore. Maybe take a couple of days and stay in town. It would be easier to think not in his environment.

"Mama, I am thinking about going into town for a couple of days to stay. Would that be okay?"

"Yes, I think it is a wonderful idea. It will get your mind off missing my son. There are a couple of really good paradors with great views of the town. It is a safe place to visit. My favorite parador is the Santa Catalina parador—it holds views of the city and countryside. Please do let Javier know where you go."

"I will let Javier know I am going away for a few days. I am feeling better already."

"I told you the tea would heal you up."

"You are very wise. I appreciate that we had this talk."

"I am here for you. I do hope you will consider what I said about settling down with Javier."

"I will consider it." With that Olivia got up and left the library. She had a new adventure to take.

Chapter 23

"Being deeply loved by someone gives you strength, while loving someone deeply gives you courage." ~ Lao Tzu

It was a forgone conclusion that he and Olivia would make a great married couple. Now he just needed to convince her to listen. He'd not helped his own case back in Barbados when he foolishly said he was not the marrying kind of man. At the time, he never thought he'd want to spend his life with the same person, mostly because he thought he'd never meet anyone as special and put together as Olivia. They'd met by accident. The more he pondered how fate had set him up, the more he realized he owed a debt of gratitude to that woman and baby in the airport store.

He now had the woman of his dreams, his Olivia. She was so raw and real, never shying away from saying what needed to be said. And she spoke what he needed to hear too.

Yet she was also vulnerable and gave her heart. The way she interacted with his family melted him. She cared about him. She cared about them. Olivia was just pure love for people. He could now see why her novels were so popular. They exuded love. No, she'd poured love into her characters and people wanted to escape their problems to live inside her words made real on the page. He'd seen it for himself when he made good on his promise to read her first book, the one for Jane—reading it nonstop on one of his mission trips. It had made him feel close to Olivia even as he missed being next to her.

She really was like his next breath—alive, refreshing and intoxicating. He'd marry her or keeping stalking her till she said yes and they sealed the deal. Making love and having her at the palazzo while Mama healed was enough for now, even though she was a handful refusing to entertain his proposal. He was not going to bring it up again until he was sure she was ready to say yes. He would be patient and wait for her to trust the love she held for him. After all, they had a lifetime together...

Javier pulled his car into the palazzo's garage midmorning, exhausted and needing some sleep. He hadn't called home to tell them today was the day he would return. Who knew if today was going to be 'the day' just in case he could not get home for another day or week. He was already feeling guilty for leaving both Mama and Olivia while he went off to work. At the time, it could not be helped or so he thought at that moment. Now he wasn't so sure. He had some idea the intensity of his feelings for Olivia, but the trip had been unbearable without her. The weather on the East Coast was touch and go with storms and fog; he had been up around the clock for two days traveling. Even though he'd helped rescue the missing crew of a fishing boat, he was determined to get back home and lay next to his Olivia as soon as possible.

What's a few more hours he kept saying to himself? Finally, he'd made it and there were just a few more steps to go until he was in her presence again. All he wanted was one of Olivia's hugs and a few kisses. Or maybe to make love to her and then sleep for days! He and Olivia had been inseparable for many weeks, and he'd surmised before his trip that a break would give her space to miss him and agree to his marriage proposal. He also wanted to squash the thought that he might begin to tire from holding her in his arms, and making love to her night after night. Even without her body, he had not stopped craving the private smiles she would give him across the room, the voice of reason she spoke when his mind was made up, the sound of her voice. Every free moment he'd had, he found himself dialing in to check and see what she was doing, if she was okay, if she had written a new chapter in her book. Out of sight, was not out of mind! Boy, whoever made up that saying was wrong!

Being away, he realized he loved Olivia more than ever and he would do whatever it took to marry her. Javier hoped he would not live to regret leaving her alone to consider his proposal. The first order of business after sleep was to rearrange his work schedule. He didn't have to work so much, he'd chosen to be available. When it was just him, he felt a sense of duty to go help people in need; especially if others could stay at home with their families. If he left Olivia's side again, they'd be husband and wife, and she'd have his promise never to be gone for long—a promise he would keep until death parted them!

After leaving the garage, he let himself into the garden, hoping to find her there in one of her favorite spots. Nope. He went through the nearest door on the back of the house, the library. The library was another favorite. She was not there either. Where is she? It was middle of the morning, so few people would be around until afternoon siesta. Morning time was when Olivia loved to be in the garden so she could work on her romance novel uninterrupted.

Surely she must be resting – it would be a treat to find her in his bed! Just the thought excited him and all thoughts of exhaustion evaporated. Javier raced up the backstairs two at a time and didn't run into anyone on the way. The back staircase leads directly to his suite of rooms and no one really ever uses it, except him and Olivia. They'd joked that it was their secret hideaway in a house too big to find anyone without taking a lap.

He opened the door, and she was not there in the sitting room, nor did he find her in the office, bedroom or bathrooms. Where is she? Has she gone out shopping for the day? Has something happened? His family seemed to love her and she was fitting right in, or so he'd thought. He stopped to look at his phone. Olivia had not left him a message. He dialed her cell phone. It did not ring. Instead it went directly to voicemail and he decided not to leave a message. Javier walked through

all the rooms and Olivia was nowhere to be found...
Something was definitely wrong and he did not have a
good feeling about it. Now what? I know who will
know—Mama!

Desperate after finding Olivia gone, Javier went in
search of his mother. If Olivia or anyone moved five
steps, Mama would know! Nothing happened at the
palazzo that she didn't have a hand in, even if she was
recovering from illness. He found his mother in the front
study, sitting in a chair with her feet propped up, and a
blanket over her legs. She was reading a book, yet she
looked tired.

"Mama, where is Olivia?" Javier said not bothering to
greet his mother or make small talk. He loved his mother
but he wanted to see Olivia now. He wanted to make
sure everything was okay.

His mother stopped staring at the book, and looked up at
Javier. "Oh, you're back! Well hello my workaholic
son!"

Not walking into the not so hidden innuendo, Javier
said, "Si, Buenos Dias Mama! How are you? Where is
Olivia?"

In a matter of fact voice, Javier heard her say, "I'm fine.
She's not here. She left for a retreat."

Javier stared at his mother as if she'd grown a second head. "What! When did she leave? I talked to her early yesterday and she didn't mention leaving or taking a retreat!"

His mother sighed and then continued to speak, "Olivia looked exhausted when I asked her to have tea with me yesterday morning. We had a little chat. She said that since you've been gone she hadn't been sleeping well. She really missed you and said she wanted some time away to think. You all are grown, so I didn't think I should tell her not to go or that she should stay or even what to do. So, for the most part, I listened. Yesterday afternoon after asking a few questions about the city of Jaen, she decided to go explore. She left the palazzo before dinner and told me not to worry. She also mentioned she'd let you know that she was going away and would be back in a couple of days."

Exasperated and finding it hard to believe that Mama kept her opinion to herself, he said, "Mama you had no right to meddle in my relationship with Olivia."

His mother frowned and pursed her lips together. "I did not meddle in your relationship. If I did, I have every right! You're my son and I want you to be happy."

"Well she's gone, and I'm not happy." He said as he paced back and forth in front of her chair.

Mama looked up at her son and said, "Olivia needed to do what she needed to do. Look, I am under no illusion. I've spoiled all of my sons and they are not easy to get along with. You are not easy to get along with mi hijo. If she's the right one for you, and I think she is, then she has to do for herself what it takes to realize it."

He ran his hands through his hair. Looking defeated and feeling the weight of no sleep on his psyche, he said. "Oh Mama, you forced this. How could you?"

"No Javier, you set this course when you brought Olivia here to your childhood home, to me! And then you proposed marriage to her, and left her with us while you went off to save the world. Not that I am complaining. She is a lovely woman with just the recipe to wear you down and conquer your heart. But she has to realize it on her own and freely choose you. It would not be right to tell her what to choose, and that includes you my dear child."

It was Javier's turn to sigh. Then he dropped his tall and stressed body to sit down on the ottoman where his mother rested her feet. "Oh Mama, I screwed up! I cannot blame you for my actions, for leaving, for putting too much pressure on Olivia too fast. I thought she would be happy to get married. I proposed and she would not say yes. I thought she would say yes by the time I came back. I didn't want to let her get away from me. I want to spend my life with her." He put his head in his hands as if he was defeated.

Mama gently rubbed Javier's back as she had done countless times as her sons had grown up and offered words of comfort. "It's going to work out. Yes, you might have screwed up with Olivia. The good news is you are still alive so you have plenty of opportunity to clean up whatever you messed up. I do not believe you put too much pressure on her. She is worthy of you!"

"Oh Mama, I hope you are right."

"Look at me, mi hijo." Javier lifted his head and turned toward his mother. She reached out and cupped her son's strong jaw with her right hand. Looking into the depth of his soul, she spoke. "Olivia is very strong willed and a brilliant woman. She has to choose her own destiny in her own good time. You are pursuing your love, giving your heart freely and I'm proud of you for going after her. It is in not taking a chance that is the ultimate failure. And I did not raise any of you to ever stop pursuing what you want! Failure is not an option. Olivia loves you and let you bring her halfway around the world to meet your family. Trust that she will choose forever with you and that real love will overcome all!"

"Thank you Mama."

"You're welcome my dear. You know what there is to do? Go find her, make amends and let her choose freely. Now shoo, I need to finish reading my book."

"Si Mama, you are always right. I am going to go find her and bring her home." Javier gave his mom a big hug and left her to her reading as she'd requested...he had a new sense of purpose that was not given by guilt but by unbounding love for his Olivia. He would find her...

******

"Maybe we aren't ready to settle down yet?" Pacing back and forth in front of the window, he stopped and turned to face his brother, Juan Carlos.

Getting a blank stare, he raised his hands in exasperation. "Has everyone lost all common sense?"

"Javier, calm down, she has not left Spain. What did her note say?"

"Why does it matter? It doesn't say much. Where could she have gone?"

"Sorry man, it was not my job to watch her. Can I see the note?"

He threw the paper across the few yards that separated them and they both watched it float to the floor to land at Juan Carlos' feet. With amusement he could barely contain, Juan Carlos lifted the paper.

Javier, if you are reading this, then you are back and know I've left the palazzo. I have been debating back

267

and forth. I needed some time to myself to think and consider your proposal. I will be back in a few days. Being there I could think of no one else but you. I promise to have answer for you when I return.

"Well, she says she needs a few days to think, is considering your proposal, and will be back. What has you so upset?" Juan Carlos looked up from the paper and saw the worried look in Javier's eyes, the paleness in his face. "This is serious. What proposal, Javier? What made that beautiful woman flee needing space?"

In true Javier fashion, he ran his hand through his hair as if composing himself to speak. "I asked Olivia to marry me."

"And? What did she say?"

Looking defeated, he sighed. "She said it was too soon to be asking her that question."

"Oh, I see."

"Do you? Cause I don't."

"Look, I know you are used to getting what you want when you want it. When it comes to women, you cannot be a bull in the China shop."

"What's that supposed to mean? Olivia is smart, beautiful, sexy; she and I are perfect together, she gets

268

along with my family, I love her. I will have her as my wife."

"Did you tell her she would be your wife like you just told me?"

"Of course not. I am not stupid. I know my heart, and it beats for her. I asked her to marry me. I know she has had her heart broken in the past. I have been patient and need her here so she too can see this is meant to be."

"Oh, so you can manipulate her, you mean? What are you afraid of? She said she will be back. If you two are meant to be as you say, then it will work out."

"Yeah, that's easy for you to say since you are married to Lacey, and all happy."

"Well, I had my doubts that she would say yes. You cannot compare my relationship to yours. You brought your woman home to your family. I married mine before she ever met you all."

"You are not helping." He turned to look out the window. "She is my heart. I worry that she is alone in my home country, she might be upset."

Juan Carlos came up behind him and slapped him on the back. "Love does crazy stuff to us. This might be hard, and you have to respect her request. She will come back to you with an answer."

Javier wanted Juan Carlos to be right. In the meantime, he needed to find her.

Chapter 24

"From this day forward, you shall not walk alone. My heart will be your shelter, and my arms will be your home." ~ Anonymous

Olivia had been a tourist for a day in Jaen. She loved this town. She had wondered what it would have been like to wander through the streets with Javier versus being alone. She'd had time to think too.

Now she was back in her room at the parador. It was such a quiet place that she found solace in doing her work. She heard a knock at the door and set her laptop on the coffee table. She was not expecting room service. She went to the door and looked out. It was the Pilot.

She opened the door. "Hi Javier. You're back?"

"Yes, I came home to find you gone. I did find your note."

"I meant to call, leave a message, but I just needed a couple of days." She turned and walked back to the sofa and sat down. She put the computer back on her lap and pretending to be typing.

"Why are you always hiding behind your work?"

Olivia looked up from her laptop. He could see she was irritated and he did not care. He wanted her full attention, needed her to listen to his point of view.

She sighed. "Really Javier, you do not want to pick this battle. You of all people should know better than to question the amount of time I work. You literally just arrived back from being gone a week."

"That's different. I was out saving lives."

"Yes, an admirable profession. And I am making people happy with my writing and it is what I like to do." She set the laptop aside, and gave him her full attention. "I get you missed me. Do you want to share what's really going on and why you're here?"

"What are you talking about?"

"I know you well enough to know there is something on your mind. You have my attention. Do you care to share it, or are we gonna have a tit for tat argument? I will let you decide the easy way or the hard way. This one though, I promise I will win. And if I win, you are not going to like it."

He weighed his options and knew Olivia would make good on what she said. That was one thing he could count on, she kept her word.

"Every time you walk out the door, I turn into an emotional basket case. I don't even know why. One minute I feel strong and in control of my feelings and the next, I am ready to roll up into a ball and cry. What am I really afraid of? Do I believe you are too good to be true? Are you too good to be true Javier?"

He ran his hands through his hair. "Bella mia, why do you do this to yourself. Why do you doubt us? I have done nothing but express my feelings for you. They are true and real. I might not know the right thing to say or how do you say? Um say it in the right way. And here I am trying to convince you that what we have is special, it is worth fighting for, turning my life upside down to win and keep your heart."

"I do not want to fight." She said as she bit her lip.

"Then stop resisting what you feel. Love me freely and without reservation."

"What if it doesn't work, what if we don't work?"

He laughed out loud. "Really Olivia how do you say that with a straight face? Us not work? Impossible. We cannot keep our hands off each other. We are in the same room sharing secret looks and messages that no one else can understand. We talk, we dance, we have a connection that so few have. When I hold you in my arms, all I want to do is please you, give you whatever you desire, make love to you and damn everything else. You know I am right."

"What if I don't want you to be right?"

"You cannot help it. What's happening between us will never change. We will never tire of each other or get bored. Come here Olivia, please?" The look of desperation he gave her melt her heart.

"Querida, there is nothing to fight. I am not going anywhere. It will never be any different for us. The same thing that was so powerful that drew us together when we met, it is not to be quenched."

She saw the pure love in his gaze.

"Olivia, nothing about the past, mine or yours, means anything to me. Here we are now. I asked you to marry me so we give our word to something, we risk all we say we were for what is possible. Anything is possible for us."

He laid his forehead against hers. She sighed and put the palms of her hands on his chest. "Javier, all I need is you."

He lifted his head from hers, put his finger under her chin to lifted her gaze to his. "And all I need is you. Say yes to me now and forever Olivia. Be my wife, my partner, my everything?"

"Yes."

He titled his head to the side. Unsure how to take her simple yes. Was he dreaming? Could this woman, his woman, have just given herself over to him.

"Really, yes?"

"Yes, Javier. I will marry you. You had my heart all this time. It's time to give my word to you, my commitment and to create our future. There's no reason to fight for control of something I never had any control over in the first place. You make me smile and laugh, and I never want to leave your side. When you are near me, I am so distracted. Can't think straight. I could listen to your voice all day long and never tire. I love you and we make great partners, in and out of bed."

"From nothing and with love, we will make this relationship up as we go. Our pasts are complicated, rocky, and it brings us to this day, here now in the moment together. If we look backwards, we will not go forward. If we long for someday, we miss out on today." Javier smiled and the twinkle of passion was right there. He bent down on one knee, opened the ring box that held the precious Tiffany cut diamond surrounded by sapphires. She stuck out her left hand, and he places the ring on her shaking finger.

"Querida, there is no reason to be nervous. I am right here by your side to cherish you each moment. I will take care of you always, cherish and love you with all that I am. You are all that is good in me and you have the biggest part of my heart."

She cupped his face in her hands and bent to have her lips on his. Wasn't long before he was inside her and making love as if there was no tomorrow. There was only this moment of now.

******

Mama had her way or at least most of it...a wedding of her son at the palazzo. Just seven short days after Olivia had said yes, she was now his wife. He would give his life for her, ensure her every need was met, her every want granted. He looked over at her across the terrace. She was chatting and smiling with his cousins. He was amazed at how easily she let them love her and genuinely enjoyed being with people. With a family as big as his, that was a blessing. Olivia is an angel, his angel.

As if she knew he was thinking of her, she looked up at him. She mouthed "I love you, I want you now."

Being the dutiful husband that was his cue…

Epilogue

""...but I found him whom my soul loveth: I held him, and would not
let him go, until I had brought him into my mother's house..."

~ Song of Solomon 3:4

Olivia, dressed in her traveling clothes, sat down at the desk and pulled a note card from her purse. She unfolded it and looked at the blank page. She had been putting off doing this for weeks. The time was now right and appropriate. It needed to be complete before she left Spain to begin a new chapter in her life, a life with her husband.

My Dear Jane...

It has been a lifetime since you departed...I still hold you dearest in my heart, and I constantly use the lessons you once taught me to be the kind of woman you'd be proud of. I have gone on to become the author you envisioned and am blessed beyond the wildest dreams of my earliest years of life. I am out traveling the world and never forget all the good times we shared.

And I am a married woman now. I would have brought the man I love home to you, if only you had lived long enough to meet him in person. Well, here's my opportunity to introduce Javier Gutierrez to you through the writings of my hand and this pen to paper, and then to send these words into the universe from which I know your spirit still silently watches over me.

I met Javier in the airport on my way to the beach. And no, there was induction into the mile-high club on that trip. I'm still a good girl. Plus, there was no opportunity as he is a rescue pilot who saves people's lives by helicopter versus airplane.

Javier was raised in a region of Spain called Andalusia and now lives on his very own island in the Caribbean Sea. He has resources to be a partner with me so we will never starve. Even though he lives abroad, he loves family, being with his parents and all five siblings. That is rare indeed.

The island Javier and I will call home, is a beautiful place, entitled Paradise Found. There is a villa with enough bedrooms for guests and maybe babies too someday; there is even a wooden swing tied to a big tree overlooking the ocean. When I first saw the swing, I was reminded of the one we had at the old homestead when I was a child. You remember it? And all the times you'd call out from the porch to "hold on tight and swing for the heavens?" I'll have you know when no one was looking, I got on the swing and tried it out!

Anyway, you already know how much my heart was hurt in the past. So, this man was not someone I was looking for. I wasn't looking for love. Yet, Javier's kindness to me and willingness to help others is endearing. It healed me just being loved by this man for no reason, and with no expectations. I finally put aside all my

278

childish thoughts about men and being hurt. I gave real love a chance. He has my heart, now and forever more.

I have inherited a family bigger than I know what to do with or how to fit into. They are lovely people and opened their arms to me even before I realized I was in love with their son and brother.

From the other room, Olivia heard the call of her husband.

"Querida, are you ready to go?"

Olivia looked up from her writing to see her debonair husband poke his head into the room. She smiled. "Just about. Please one more minute my dear."

"Of course, take your time. I will meet you downstairs."

She nodded her assent, watched him disappear, and sighed. She then returned her attention to the letter.

Mama, I finally made it to my heaven and I'm happy...who knew one could have such peace and be settled. Alas, perhaps you blew that wind across the seas and sent Pilot Javier to me after all...for that, and for teaching me to recognize real love when he showed up in your line at the store, I say thank you...

I have to go. We leave within the hour to the airport. I'm home bound...back to Paradise Found. I promise to write again...until then goodbye my Jane...

Kisses, hugs and love always ~ your daughter, Olivia

She folded the note, placed it in an envelope that simply read '*To My Mother Jane.*' She pressed a monogram seal to its tip, and dropped it into her purse. Now I'm ready to go home...

And off she went to find the man she loved more than life itself - Pilot Javier!

The End

About the Author:

L. Elaine lives in Maryland, just outside her hometown of Washington, DC. She has three sons, a daughter-in-law, and a granddaughter, whose eyes sparkle each time she gets a new idea!

Almost a decade ago, with coaxing from a dear friend at work, she decided to write her own romance novel to see if she would enjoy crafting beautiful stories of love set in exotic locales. And she does, so she continues to write!

Besides reading and writing, L. Elaine enjoys traveling, teaching, meeting people and tasting food from foreign lands. She considers herself a lifelong learner with lots left to discover! She would love to hear from you so please visit her website.

<u>EXCERPT</u>

from the next book
in the series
Dynasty of Love

The Gutiérrez Family: Book 3

And stay tuned for more love stories from the *Dynasty of Love* series about the Gutiérrez family!

Alberto and Arabella's Story…excerpt:

After an amazing round of sex, and a quick nap, Alberto was awakened by the light being switched on. Across the room in the doorway there Arabella stood looking like an angel bearing gifts. When had she left his side?

"I brought us some food," she said as she walked into the room wearing a summer dress that accentuated every curve from her bosom, to her thin waist, and to the hips he caressed as she rode him to orgasm. Feeling his erection stir to life, he thought, damn she is beautiful, and she's mine. I want that.

She smiled at him, as if hearing his thoughts. "You hungry? I'm starving."

Not wanting to go there yet, he looked at the tray. "Where did all that come from? When did you leave?"

"Chef texted me about thirty minutes ago to let me know your mom had made her world famous lasagna and insisted on sending me some. Your mom thinks I work too much and need to eat healthier. I met him on the doorstep downstairs. Your mom sent way too much."

"She's probably right about that. You spend too many hours in the lab."

"I know, only men can be excused for working too much, right?

283

Attempting to lighten the suddenly serious mood, he said, "I didn't say that. It just leaves little time for you to cook me meals."

"That's funny," she said. Even though she did not like the idea of women being relegated to slaving over the hot flames to prepare meals for men who don't know how to come home and do their fair share, this was not a conversation for this moment. "Don't hold your breath for that. Well anyway, here is a tray for us to share." She put it down in the middle of the bed.

She looked down. "Oh, I forgot the bread. Be right back."

When she returned, she could see Alberto had made a plate and set it on his lap. "I've returned."

"Welcome back," he smiled. "So, I can get you to bring me dinner as long as someone else prepares it?"

"Yes exactly! I'm a scientist, not a chef."

"I grow olives and I like cooking. I'm good at it."

"Okay that's good news so then you won't expect me to cook for you."

He smirked, "I don't know about all that. Mama always says that the way to a man's heart is through his stomach."

She rolled her eyes at him and threw a dinner roll across the bed at him. "You are ungrateful. I am not interested in getting to your heart Alberto. As a matter of fact, I don't even know why I bothered to bring this tray. You can have your stupid stereotypes about women."

"Whoa I am only joking with you Mi Tesoro. You are so sexy when you are angry! Come here to me and I will serve you."

"I am not a lovesick puppy you can spoil."

"Oh, the things I want to do to you. I promise there is no doubt that I would ever mistake you for docile, subservient puppy or at my beck and call. Please Arabella...come eat with me. There is no point in wasting the food Mama has sent over."

"Only because I don't want to disappoint your mother, will I join you." She laid across the bed, and he scooped food on a plate for her...

Made in the
USA
Middletown, DE